"There is something I want to discuss with you."

She gazed at him with mild curiosity. *"Okey."*

Joshua ran his fingers through his hair as he strived for the right thing to say. "As you must have learned by now, I lost my wife over seven months ago."

"Ja." Her green eyes filled with sympathy. "I'm sure that has been hard."

"It has been." He paused, wondering how best to phrase his request. "My little ones need a *mam*, and, well...I'd like her to be you. But I need to be honest, Esther," he added. "What I'm offering is a marriage of convenience. If you agree to be my wife, you'll have a home with us and children to care for. I can't promise more." He swallowed against a lump in his throat. "Anything I have will be yours...except my heart. I'll understand if you say *nay*." He waited for what felt like forever for her to respond, as it had become vitally important to him that she say yes.

Rebecca Kertz was first introduced to the Amish when her husband took a job with an Amish construction crew. She enjoyed watching the Amish foreman's children at play and swapping recipes with his wife. Rebecca resides in Delaware with her husband and dog. She has a strong faith in God and feels blessed to have family nearby. Besides writing, she enjoys reading, doing crafts and visiting Lancaster County.

Books by Rebecca Kertz

Love Inspired

Loving Her Amish Neighbor
In Love with the Amish Nanny
The Widow's Hidden Past
His Forgotten Amish Love
A Convenient Christmas Wife

Women of Lancaster County

A Secret Amish Love
Her Amish Christmas Sweetheart
Her Forgiving Amish Heart
Her Amish Christmas Gift
His Suitable Amish Wife
Finding Her Amish Love

Visit the Author Profile page at LoveInspired.com for more titles.

A Convenient Christmas Wife

REBECCA KERTZ

LOVE INSPIRED
INSPIRATIONAL ROMANCE

LOVE INSPIRED®

INSPIRATIONAL ROMANCE

Recycling programs for this product may not exist in your area.

ISBN-13: 978-1-335-93683-7

A Convenient Christmas Wife

Love Inspired
22 Adelaide St. West, 41st Floor
Toronto, Ontario M5H 4E3, Canada
www.LoveInspired.com

Printed in Lithuania

MIX
Paper | Supporting responsible forestry
FSC® C021394

He healeth the broken in heart,
and bindeth up their wounds.
—*Psalms* 147:3

For Crystal... Here's to Sweet 16, Elton John
and Wonderful Memories

Chapter One

❧

Lancaster County, Pennsylvania

Esther King took one last walk-through of the house she'd cleaned from top to bottom as a favor to her employer. Fannie's widowed brother, Joshua, would be moving with his four children into the residence sometime this week. As she strolled from room to room, she was relieved to see that all the floors shone thanks to the thorough sweeping and mopping she'd done on the hardwood and vinyl flooring. The kitchen counters had been washed, and the bathroom scrubbed and sanitized. She'd stocked the kitchen with a few basics such as milk, butter, eggs and bread. Esther had also brought over two jars of homemade jam that she'd made last spring with her *mam* and sister as well as a few canned vegetables and fruit so Joshua and his children would have something to eat until he could shop for groceries.

Cleaning here was an easy job for Esther, especially since the three-bedroom, one-level home was brand-new.

Shaking herself from her thoughts, Esther gathered some of her cleaning supplies and carried them to her buggy in the side yard. Jonas would show his son the house later in the day, and she wanted to be gone well before their arrival.

After setting her broom and plastic carryall of cleaners in the back of her buggy, she returned inside to grab her mop and did one more quick check in the kitchen to make sure she hadn't left anything of hers behind. Esther stepped outside with her mop in hand. She heard a squealing meow before she tripped and landed on her hands and knees. The sound of buggy wheels in the yard made her groan as she realized that someone had seen her fall.

"Esther!" she heard somebody cry out from inside the buggy and sensed someone racing to her side to help her.

Mortified, she closed her eyes and shook her head, then looked up at Preacher Jonas Miller, who gently helped her to stand. The kind man eyed her with concern. "Are you *oll recht*?" he asked.

"I'm fine," she assured him, "but I don't know if the cat is." She had scraped her knee and elbow and bruised her hip, but she wouldn't admit that she was hurt. Embarrassed, Esther brushed off her dress and then glanced toward the vehicle as Joshua, Fannie's brother and Jonas's son, slowly swung his legs out of the buggy, his expression strained as if his every movement was painful. Fannie unfolded a walker for him, and Joshua grabbed hold of it for balance as he slid awkwardly from the buggy seat and onto his feet. He caught Esther's gaze as he slowly made his way toward his father, and she felt her face heat up. She looked at Jonas instead.

"The cat ran off so I'm sure it's *okey*." Jonas picked up her mop and handed it to her. "*Danki* for getting the *haus* ready."

Her smile for him was genuine as she took the mop. "I enjoyed it."

"Yet you don't clean houses anymore," the preacher said.

Esther nodded as her heart rate increased in painful

thumps. "I like working for Fannie in the restaurant." No one, not even her family, knew the real reason she'd decided to give up her business.

One morning, she'd arrived at a housecleaning job only to leave within minutes because she'd been suffering from unbearable abdominal cramps. Esther had been able to get a doctor's appointment that same day, especially after confessing that she'd been having cramps for over two months and these had been the worst of them. The doctor had examined her and ordered tests. When the results came back, the woman had given her bad news. Esther suffered from endometriosis, a medical condition that typically made women infertile. She would never get the chance to give birth or hold her baby in her arms. Since then, she'd had difficulty accepting she'd never have children. She still couldn't quite accept it, as she had always longed to be a wife and mother.

"I should get home." She turned to head toward her vehicle, then stopped at the sight of Joshua Miller, braced on his walker, standing in her way. She froze and stared at him, taken aback by how attractive he was.

"Joshua," his father said, "this is Esther King. She got the *haus* ready for you."

The man studied her through narrowed eyes for a long minute but didn't speak.

Esther averted her gaze and, anxious to leave, moved to pass him. "I should get home. I'll see you at work tomorrow, Fannie." She walked toward her buggy.

"Can you give me a lift to my *dat*'s?" Fannie asked. "Alta has the children and I want to be there to assist her. Just give me a minute."

"*Okey*," Esther said with a nod. Alta and Jonas's house sat on the front acreage of their farm, which was on a different road. Esther knew the preacher had bought the unfin-

ished shell of a *dawdi haus* from another Amish property
owner who had sold the main house to *Englishers*. Jonas
had purchased it and had it moved to this location in the
rear of their property, far enough from Jonas's house for
privacy yet close enough in case Joshua needed help.

Conscious of her friend's brother within several feet of
her, Esther moved to wait near her buggy while Fannie
spoke quietly with her father before heading in her direction.

"Esther." The deep male voice was unfamiliar. Joshua's.

Face hot, she turned, reluctantly meeting his gaze. He
was a handsome man with dark hair—and with a hint of
what looked like sadness in his intense brown eyes.

"*Danki* for what you did here," he said. His expression
hadn't softened but he sounded sincere. She knew he suffered from loss as he recovered from the tragic accident
that had killed his wife six months ago, and she wished she
could ease his pain.

Esther nodded. "You're *willkomm*." Then she spun around
to get into her vehicle and waited until Fannie climbed in
next to her.

"Are you *oll recht*?" her friend asked as Esther drove
toward the Jonas Miller dairy farm.

"I'm fine." She shot Fannie a look. "How is he? Your
bruder?"

Fannie frowned. "He's hurting."

"I can only imagine." Unwilling to dig for more infor-
mation, she drove the rest of the way to the Millers' dairy
farm in silence. "I'll see you at work tomorrow," Esther
said when she stopped to drop off her friend. Then she
left with a wave, her thoughts focused on Joshua Miller as
she offered up a prayer for him to recover and have peace.

During the drive home from the Miller residence, she

couldn't stop thinking of the moment when she'd locked eyes with Joshua. She'd felt unsettled when faced with such a good-looking man, until he'd thanked her and the uncomfortable sensation inside her eased.

This was the first time she'd met him…and now that she had finished her work in the house, she doubted she'd have much interaction with him except for seeing him at church services here and there. Which was fine by her.

Using his walker, Joshua slowly, painfully, approached his father near the front door of the house that he and his children would be living in until he felt well enough to buy or build a bigger home. This residence was all on one level, a necessity since he was still recovering from his injuries from the car accident that had killed his pregnant wife, Anna, six months ago. He'd stayed in their home in Arthur, Illinois, all this time since the accident. He'd struggled to get well and take care of his children by himself, living in a world of hurt and grief after losing Anna and their unborn child. If not for his four motherless children, he might have given up altogether, but he loved them and needed to be there for them. After accepting the help of his former neighbors and his wife's best friend Ruth, who had assisted with his *kinner* after the accident, he'd finally realized that the best thing for him to do was to call his father and return home to New Berne to be closer to his family.

"Whose property is this?" he asked as his father held open the door for him. Joshua entered the house and stepped into the kitchen.

"It's yours," *Dat* said with a small smile.

Joshua shot his father a glance. "What do you mean it's mine?" he asked, his tone sharp.

His father placed a calming hand on his shoulder. "I'd

hoped you'd call and want to come back so I bought the un-finished *haus* and had it moved here. With the help of our church members, you now have a new place to live with a barn for your buggy and animals. I know about your loss, soohn. It's *gut* that you came. Our family can help you through this."

He felt the weight of his grief and responsibilities. "Dat, I'll pay you back."

"*Nay*," his *dat* said. "Live in it for a year or more until you know if you want a larger *haus*. I'll sell it or give it to you, depending on where you want to stay. But there is no need to decide now. If you want to live elsewhere, that's fine. Alta and I may one day want a one-level house." He grinned. "But not yet." He gestured around the room. "Take a look. If you don't think this will work for you, that's *okey*. I don't want you to live somewhere you're not comfortable."

Studying his surroundings, Joshua awkwardly made his way farther into the kitchen. He saw beautifully built cabi-nets, shiny countertops…and a vase of fresh fall flowers on the kitchen table. His gaze locked on the blooms, and he suffered a pang as he recalled how much Anna had loved flowers in their home.

"The flowers are Esther's doing. She loves growing them in her family's greenhouse." His *vadder* grinned. "You'll find everything clean and ready for someone to move in right away." His father opened the pantry then stepped back to show him.

Swallowing a lump in his throat, he met his parent's gaze. "Who is she?" He had a lasting impression of blond hair beneath her *kapp* and green eyes set in lovely features with a small nose and nicely shaped lips.

"Esther?" his *dat*'s smile was soft. "She's Adam and

Lovina King's youngest daughter. She has a sister, Linda, and three *bruders*."

He blinked and looked away. "Why did she clean for us? Why her?"

"Esther used to own a housecleaning business," *Dat* said as he leaned against the counter, drawing Joshua's attention. "She gave it up and now works for your sister at her luncheonette."

"I don't understand why she would give it up." Joshua moved to the vase and lightly touched the largest bloom among many, a bright red gerbera daisy. "She's *gut* at it."

"I have no idea why." Jonas pushed off the counter until he reached his son's side. "She seemed happy at her job until one day she told her parents she didn't want to do it anymore. She'd been working part-time for Fannie back then whenever she had time as a side job to her business. Esther wanting full-time work turned out great for your *schweschter*, who had added catering to her business and needed more full-time workers." His *dat* walked through the kitchen and into the living room, where he stood waiting patiently for Joshua to follow. In the living room, there was a sofa, four chairs with two matching upholstered ottomans, as well as side tables and a storage chest.

Pushing aside what he'd learned about the shy young woman, Joshua studied the large space where he and his children could enjoy a Sunday afternoon. "This is a nice-size room."

His father nodded. "There are three bedrooms and a bathroom with a washing machine and a dryer. I bought the place from a family who sold their two-story home. The *dawdi haus* on the property was available, and we didn't have to move it far from their place to this plot on the far side of ours." He studied the living room before glancing back at him. "Let me show you everything."

Struggling with the walker, Joshua started to trail his *dat*.

Dat gestured toward the contents of the first bedroom as he stepped inside, and Joshua entered behind him. There was a large bed, a dresser, two bed tables and wall hooks next to the right side of the door. "The original plans had this space as the only bedroom but the *haus* was never finished."

Joshua liked it. The room had hardwood floors and a lovely quilt covering the bed. "Nice quilt. One of Alta's?"

"*Nay.* I don't recognize it. I'm not sure where it came from," his father said, "but I wouldn't be surprised if Esther is responsible."

After nodding in approval, Joshua left the room and waited for his father to exit.

"We added two other bedrooms and this bathroom to the main structure." Jonas smiled as he showed him the bathroom with a tub-shower combination, toilet and sink. Towels hung on a rack between the sink and the shower. There was a solid blue shower curtain, pushed to the side and allowing a view of the inside. The new fixtures glistened as if Esther had just cleaned and polished them. Along the outer wall was a gas-generated washing machine that vented to the outside.

Joshua studied the room and noted the kerosene lamp hung over the sink.

His father urged him onward and stepped inside the next bedroom. "Two cribs for your twins."

He experienced a pang as he saw the baby furniture. "They recently turned two. I have a feeling they won't be able to sleep in a crib for much longer."

"I thought of that," his *dat* replied. "The cribs can be taken apart and made into toddler beds."

"That's *gut*," Joshua said, pleased. "Did you make them?"

"Our neighbor Gabriel Fisher built them." He beamed at Joshua. "He's a talented woodworker. He makes toys as well as furniture. He has a couple of young ones of his own."

Joshua hobbled with his walker behind his father as he entered the last and final bedroom. There were two single beds inside. This room, like the others, was large and left a lot of space for children to play or relax. He felt a welcoming frisson of pleasure as hope filled his heart that he and his *kinner* would eventually be happy here. Being close to his father and his family was the best decision he'd made since Anna's death.

A repetitive knocking on the back door drew the two of them back into the kitchen. His *dat* opened it, and Joshua was startled to see Esther King outside, shifting uneasily. He felt something odd settle inside him as she entered the house, and he studied her from the other side of the room.

"I'm sorry to bother you, Preacher." She cast a worried glance in Joshua's direction. "I think I left something in one of the bedrooms."

"Come in," his father replied kindly.

"Danki." Esther met his gaze and looked quickly away. "I'll be but a moment."

Joshua frowned as she scurried by him toward the bedrooms at the back of the house. She was gone only seconds.

"Found it!" She smiled. "I need to stop at Kings General Store but then I couldn't find my change purse." She held it up to show them. "I left it in the room with the twin beds." To Joshua's surprise, she met his gaze. "How do you like the *haus*?"

"It's the right size for us." He noticed her pretty features, her bright green eyes and dark blond hair. Joshua immediately felt guilty for noticing anything about her as his late wife suddenly filled his thoughts. "The quilts on the beds," he said politely, shoving back his grief. "Did you buy them for us?"

Esther shook her head. "*Nay.* They are some of mine. I like to quilt from time to time. I was happy to have someplace to put them."

"You made them?" Amazed at her skill, he raised his eyebrows.

"*Ja.*" She appeared amused, and the expression looked good on her.

Joshua felt a sudden headache. "How much do I owe you?"

"I don't want money for them. My thoughts on payment are if you can use them, then you do."

"That's kind of you, Esther," his father said.

The young woman seemed uncomfortable with the current topic of conversation.

"They are beautiful, Esther," Joshua said, remorse leaving a lump in his throat and a throbbing pain in his temple. "*Danki.* We will certainly benefit from having them. I appreciate everything you've done here. The chrysanthemums and gerbera daisies are a nice touch. The *haus* is welcoming because of you and I appreciate it."

To his relief, he saw her face clear. "You know flowers." Her smile reappeared. "It was my pleasure, Joshua." She gazed at him for a few seconds. "I'd better go. My *mam* is waiting for me to pick up groceries for her." But she didn't immediately leave. "Do you have any idea when you'll be moving in?"

"Tomorrow," Joshua told her. "I have trouble with stairs so living here will be a lot easier for me and my family."

Esther nodded and then turned to his father. "Reach out if you need anything."

"I will," his *vadder* assured her.

With one last smile for each of them, she left, and Joshua watched through the window as she climbed into her buggy and drove toward the road.

"So, you'll be ready to move in tomorrow?" his father asked.

"*Ja*. I think it's best if I do." Joshua shifted to ease the pain of standing for so long with his walker.

His *dat* nodded. "I'll call your *bruders*. They can help with the move in the morning."

It had been years since he'd seen DJ and Danny, his younger twin brothers. A sharp pain at his temple made him grimace. He couldn't release a hand to soothe it because he would lose his balance and further injure himself. "I think I'm ready to head back now."

His *dat* nodded again and preceded him to the kitchen door, where he propped it open. "Do you need help?" he asked, no doubt recognizing how Joshua was feeling.

"I can make it," he said, and meant it. Falling wasn't a healthy option with the type of injury he'd suffered. Would he ever recover and be back physically to the way he once was? His doctor at the hospital had been cautiously optimistic, but that could mean the answer was just as likely no as it was yes. Still, he would try to lean in to the optimism.

Chapter Two

Esther unlocked the back door of Fannie's Luncheonette and entered, turning the dead bolt behind her. She'd come in early to get ready for the day's customers. After switching on the kitchen lights, she turned on the oven to preheat, pulled out a couple of breakfast casseroles from the refrigerator and set them on the counter. She then went into the front dining area to see if all the table settings were in place. Assured that all was fine, she returned to the kitchen.

A sound at the back door heralded the arrival of Fannie Troyer.

"*Gut mariga,* Esther!" Fannie smiled as she entered the kitchen. "You're in earlier than expected this Monday morning."

"*Gut mariga*! I wanted to make up for being out on Friday." Esther placed the casseroles into the hot oven.

"I don't expect you to work extra when you're doing something for Joshua." Fannie placed a basket of fresh eggs on the counter. "You did such a *wunderbor* job at the *haus.* I was hoping that you could continue to clean for him twice a week. Would you consider doing that?"

"I don't know, Fannie." Esther hadn't minded getting the house ready for him, but the thought of cleaning for him regularly unnerved her. The last thing she needed was to be around a man and his children, reminding her of the family she would never have.

"I'll do what I can for him, but I feel like I can't fit it into my schedule, not with running the restaurant and needing to spend more time with my husband and daughter after we close up." Fannie began to crack eggs into a bowl. The special menu for the day was omelets, as well as the breakfast casseroles.

"Are Joshua and the children settled in the house?" Esther went to the refrigerator to pull out cheese and ham and set them on the counter close to where Fannie worked, before starting to make a large pot of coffee.

"*Ja,* they are." Fannie looked at her gratefully as Esther began to cut up the ham into perfectly small pieces for the omelets. "I believe the *haus* is just right for him and the children." She blinked back tears. "I hate that Joshua is suffering. Losing Anna and their unborn *bubbel* was brutal, and being so far from family while struggling to recover has made it more difficult for him."

Esther gasped. "His wife was pregnant?"

Fannie nodded. "*Ja.* Such terrible losses for him."

"I had no idea. It must be rough." Esther's heart broke for Joshua and his little ones.

The sound of the back door opening alerted Esther that it was probably Linda, coming into work at her usual time. To her surprise, it wasn't her sister who appeared at the entrance to the kitchen but Fannie's father.

"Why, *hallo!*" Jonas Miller smiled. "It already smells *gut* in here."

Fannie grinned. "Dat! Have you come to get breakfast?"

"I would like two servings of the sausage casserole for Alta and me, but I'm here for another reason." He locked gazes with Esther. "May I have a few moments of your time?"

Her employer nodded, encouraging Esther to slip into the front dining area with Jonas so they would have privacy. It was too early to open the restaurant.

Esther worried that she had missed something in Joshua's new residence. "Preacher, is something wrong?"

Jonas's smile made her relax. "On the contrary, you did a fine job. That's what I want to talk with you about. Would you consider cleaning my *soohn*'s *haus* for a while? I imagine twice each week will be enough. I'd say once a week, but with my four *kins kinner* living in the *haus* I know that Joshua won't be able to keep up until he fully recovers."

"Fannie mentioned it, but I'm not sure if it's a *gut* idea." Forcing herself to relax, she gave it some thought. "What if Joshua doesn't want me in his *haus*?"

"You have nothing to worry about." Jonas held her gaze as if awaiting her answer. "He's unable to do much. I know he'll be grateful for your help."

"I'll do what I can." How could she say no to the church elder?

"*Wunderbor!*" He appeared pleased. "I'll be the one paying you."

Esther shook her head. "*Nay.* It doesn't seem right to take your money. You have done so much for our community. I just want to help. It's the least I can do."

"I insist," Jonas said. "You'll be taking the time to take care of my *soohn*'s home, and I won't take *nay* for an answer."

She widened her eyes after he told her the amount he wanted to pay her. "Jonas, that's too much."

"You might feel differently the first time you go over to clean." Jonas grinned.

"That's more than generous. Let me clean for the first time, and we can discuss a fee then, *ja*?"

The sound of the back door opening again caught their attention. *"Hallo!"*

She grinned as she heard Linda's voice. "My *schweschter*," Esther said. "I need to check on the casseroles in the oven. Two servings of sausage, *ja*? Today we also have a casserole with both sausage and bacon."

"Sausage is fine," he said. *"Danki."* He followed her into the kitchen.

Linda saw him and smiled. "It's nice to see you, Jonas."

The preacher's lips curved. "It's *gut* to see you." He waited patiently as Esther checked the oven. The cheese atop the sausage casserole was bubbling. He addressed his daughter. "Fannie, she agreed."

Esther saw her friend's smirk. "That's *wunderbor! Danki,* Esther."

"Just what did my *schweschter* agree to?" Linda asked as she cut up peeled potatoes into small chunks for home fries.

"To clean my *bruder*'s *haus* twice a week," Fannie said with delight.

"It's nothing." Brushing the attention aside, Esther cut two large pieces of the casserole and put them in aluminum take-out containers then gave them to Jonas.

Feeling her sister's gaze, she made eye contact as she shifted closer. "I'm concerned about losing hours at the restaurant," Esther murmured for her sister's ears only.

Linda nodded as if she understood. "I'll cover for you whenever you have to work and I'm not on the schedule."

Esther beamed at her. *"Danki."*

Two days later, Esther drove her buggy into Joshua's yard, parked and gathered her cleaning supplies from the back seat. Carrying what she could hold, she approached the house and knocked on the door softly. Jonas had given her a key, but still, she wanted to be mindful of entering someone else's house without their knowledge. She waited a few moments and then finally used the key to unlock the door. She stayed outside with the door cracked open a little and called Joshua's name.

"*Hallo?* Joshua? It's Esther. I've come to clean your *haus*!" She heard a rhythmic thumping sound and stepped back from the door while waiting for him to appear.

He seemed irritable as he swung it wide open. "*What?*"

With an effort, Esther continued to smile. "I'm here to clean for you. I thought Fannie or your *vadder* would have told you…" Her hold on her cleaning supplies tightened. "But if this isn't a *gut* time, I can come back later." She turned to leave.

"It's fine," he said, holding himself up with his walker, and she spun around to meet his gaze. She could see the pain in his eyes and his tightened jaw.

She felt bad for him. "If you're sure…"

"*Ja.*" Joshua turned and moved carefully toward the kitchen table, where he pulled out a chair and sat.

Avoiding his gaze, she eased inside and set her cleaning supplies on the kitchen counter before heading outside for the rest of what she needed. Esther returned with her dry and wet mops, a bucket that held sponges, rags and a bottle of lemon oil and a spray can of furniture polish. She loved the size of his house, especially the kitchen.

"How long is this going to take?" he asked after she came back inside. With his dark hair and features, he looked like a younger version of his father.

She could tell that he didn't want her here. It was quiet in the house. Too quiet for a house with children. "I can check all the rooms if you want. If they're clean, I'll leave and return another day." Had he and the children used the quilts she'd made? She'd spent a lot of time sewing them as a teenager when she thought she'd have a husband and a family one day. Any hope of that had died when she'd learned that she couldn't have children. No man within the Amish community would want an infertile wife.

Joshua shook his head. "Go ahead and clean. This is a *gut* time. The children are with Alta."

Which only confirmed what she'd thought because of the silence. She dragged her eyes away from his startlingly handsome face. "*Oll recht.*" She lifted her bucket into the sink and turned on the tap to fill it with water.

"I expect my *kinner* to return after lunch," Joshua's voice rumbled from the kitchen table behind her.

With a nod, she shut off the faucet, put the bucket on the floor and added an all-purpose floor cleaner to the water. "I'll start with the bedrooms and bathroom, then do the living room. I'll finish with the kitchen. Will you be *oll recht* here for a while? Is there anything I can get you?" She saw the pot of coffee on the stove. "I can bring you another cup of coffee if you'd like."

"*Nay*, I'm fine." His expression softened a little before it turned hard again.

He watched her without a word, as if he wanted her to get moving so that she could be done and then gone. She averted her gaze as she grabbed the bucket, furniture polish and soft cloths and entered the living room. There were toys scattered on the hardwood floor. Fearing that Joshua would trip on them, she gathered and placed them in the basket in the corner of the living room, which held a few other playthings.

Esther dusted the furniture then used lemon oil on the oak pieces before she proceeded toward the other rooms at the back of the house. She started with the bathroom, cleaning the fixtures and mopping the floor before she moved on. The littlest ones' room was easy to clean. She smiled as her gaze settled on the baby-size quilts that hung over the side of each crib. The colors she'd used to make them were yellow and blue, and the material of each one was the same but the patterns were different.

Everything looked tidy, and Esther couldn't help but wonder why Jonas had thought his son needed her to clean twice a week. After she dusted the dresser and furniture, she mopped the vinyl floor. The furniture oil and floor cleaner lent the air a fresh lemon scent. As she left the room, she lingered in the doorway to gaze at the cribs with a fierce longing for what she would never have before she moved into the room with the two single beds.

Esther grinned when she saw clothes on the mattresses. The small dresses were bright in color. It looked like the room she'd shared with her sister when she and Linda were small and needed to be reminded to hang up their garments. She placed them on the hangers, which she hung on wall hooks. The quilts she'd brought for this room had been pulled up to cover the pillows. After ensuring that the room was tidy and neat, she dusted the furniture and cleaned the floor.

The last room she entered was the main bedroom that had been part of the original plans for the unfinished *dawdi haus* before Jonas purchased it and had it moved. She studied Joshua's unmade bed for a moment, with the homemade quilt of various shades of blue looking as if it had been tossed aside in a hurry. There were clothes scattered about on the bottom of the bed and on the floor below the wall hooks. She hung up Joshua's garments before she straightened the covers. A cane leaned against the wall in the far corner, and her first thought was he would use it once he was healed enough that he wouldn't need to rely on his walker.

After one last check to ensure the back rooms were spotless, Esther returned to the kitchen. Joshua sat in a chair, bent over the table, his head cradled in his hands. "Joshua, are you *oll recht*?"

He immediately straightened. "You finished the other rooms?"

She nodded as she set the bucket on the floor. "Would you like to move into the living room? I can make you something to eat if you'd like."

"I'm not hungry." He stood and reached for his walker. "I'll wait there until you're done."

"*Okey.*" Watching as he struggled toward the other room, she wished she could do more for him. He stopped and glanced back at her, and she quickly averted her gaze and busied herself with cleaning.

Joshua sat in a chair with his legs propped up on an upholstered ottoman. He was impatient to be alone again. He didn't like anyone seeing how weak he was…especially the young woman who was cleaning in the next room. Sighing, he closed his eyes and attempted to will away the pain. He rubbed his left leg to ease the throbbing.

Despite what he was going through, it helped knowing he lived close to his family again. After living in Manheim about a half hour away from his family home in the early years of their marriage, he and Anna had moved to Arthur in Illinois to be closer to her mother, his wife's only living relative. Sadly, within three years of their move, his mother-in-law had become ill and passed away.

Recalling the coffeepot on the stove, he decided he wanted another cup after all. Joshua struggled to his feet, using his hand to shove away his footrest so he could reach for his walker. It was slow going, and after walking less than halfway across the room, his left leg ached so badly that he regretted not staying put. Deciding that he didn't want coffee that badly after all, he returned to his chair and sat down, placing his walker within easy reach before he propped his legs up again. Leaning back, he closed his eyes, his thoughts returning to his deceased wife.

Pregnant with twins when her mother died, Anna had refused to eat more than a couple of bites at each meal during the weeks that followed. Joshua had grown increasingly worried about her health and the health of the babies she carried. And he'd been right to be concerned, since the birth of the twins had been extremely difficult for her two months later. Her doctors had thought she wouldn't be able to conceive again, that it would be risky if she did. Nearly losing her and their babies had scared him. When, against all odds, Anna became pregnant again a year later, her obstetrician had insisted they consult with a specialist who dealt with high-risk pregnancies. It didn't matter that she'd been only carrying one child. The twins' birth the year before had damaged Anna's uterus. Joshua had made an appointment with a maternal-fetal medicine specialist. The doctor's office had been located over an hour and a half away—too far for a buggy ride, so he'd hired a car and a driver to take them there.

Joshua readjusted his legs on the ottoman. He'd thought he'd done the right thing in following the doctor's orders to ensure Anna would have a healthy pregnancy and the baby she carried would be delivered safely. *But I lost them anyway.*

On the way home from the appointment, a drunk driver struck the vehicle, killing Anna instantly. Their driver was slightly wounded, and Joshua's left leg was fractured and his right leg broken, both with contusions and cuts. The time he'd spent in the hospital was terrible. He was in excruciating pain while grieving for his wife. He felt guilty, responsible for Anna's death and worried about his children, who had stayed with family within their Amish community while he and Anna had ridden to the doctor's office. The same family, along with two others, had stepped up to take care of his children until his release. Their driver's insurance had covered his medical bills with a separate amount allocated to him for his wife's death, but nothing could help with the pain of the loss he still suffered.

"Joshua." Esther stood in the archway between the living room and the hallway that led to other parts of the house. "I'm finished. Is there anything I can do for you before I leave?"

He met and held her gaze, noticing how green her eyes were. "*Nay.*"

"I'll be back in a few days." He saw her look at his elevated legs.

Joshua averted his glance. "I don't know if that will be necessary."

"I promised your *vadder* and Fannie that I'd come twice a week." She appeared uncomfortable when he returned his attention to her. "If you don't need me when I return, I'll leave."

He shifted his leg and winced as pain hammered from his left thigh to his foot. "How much do I owe you?"

Esther shook her head. "Nothing. It's taken care of."

"I pay my way," he insisted.

"You'll have to discuss this with your *vadder.*" She eyed the walker he'd set beside the chair. "Can I help you to the kitchen?"

He scowled. "I can get back by myself." Joshua immediately regretted his tone when he saw her hurt expression. "*Danki.* I appreciate what you've done. I'm sorry I'm irritable—my legs are bothering me."

Her features softened. "I understand." He got lost in the bright green of her eyes again and felt guilty for noticing them when his beloved wife was dead. "Do you have a cell phone?" she asked.

Joshua shook his head.

"You may want to get one in case of an emergency," she said softly.

And then she left the room, and moments later he heard the back door open and shut. Only silence remained to keep him company. A silence that disturbed him with memories that pained him.

Chapter Three

Fannie entered the kitchen from the back rooms of Joshua's house. "I put JJ and Jacob down for their naps. Magda and Leah are playing quietly in their room. I'll be at Adam King's house for Visiting Day. Maybe next time, you'll feel well enough to join us." She grabbed a box from her bag and handed it to him. "It's a new cell phone. Our bishop has given his permission for you to have one for emergencies. *Dat* bought it." She grabbed her bag and slung it over one shoulder. "My number is already programmed in. So is Esther's."

Joshua raised his eyebrows. "Why hers?"

His sister shook her head as if she found the simple question ridiculous. "Because she cleans your *haus*. You may need her sooner than scheduled, and she can let you know if she is running late." She smiled. "Call me if you need me."

He managed to return his sister's smile. She was always there for him and had been since he arrived in New Berne. "*Danki,* Fannie. I've taken too much of your time."

"*Nay,* Joshua. You're my *bruder* and I love you. I will always have time for you." Fannie regarded him with warmth. "Are you sure you don't want me to take your *kinner* with me? I'll keep an eye on them."

You and everyone else in the community, except me.

He missed his children whenever they weren't with him. *Something must change.* He didn't want them away from him for hours or what seemed like days at a time. He understood that his family thought he needed time to rest and recover, but being with his young'uns made him feel better.

"Go," he urged her after managing a grin. "Have fun visiting the Kings. We'll be fine. Say *hallo* to your husband." His sister had married David Troyer last year and was happier than he'd ever seen her.

Joshua rose from his chair and carefully made his way to the coffeepot on the stove. He poured himself a cup, added the fixings he liked and secured a lid onto the metal mug so that he wouldn't spill coffee as he hobbled to his favorite chair in the living room. Once seated, he swiped open the sipping hole in the plastic lid and took a sip before he set the cup on the small table next to him. It had been difficult enough dressing himself this morning. The last thing he needed was to have to change his shirt and pants because he'd spilled coffee on them. With a sigh, he put up his feet and leaned back, closing his eyes. He could hear his older children playing in their bedroom.

After finishing the brew, he made himself get up to check on his children. He had to move slowly since he still relied on his walker. Joshua felt that his recovery was taking too long. Perhaps he should consult a doctor here in New Berne and see what a specialist had to say.

Looking in on his two-year-old twins first, he smiled when he saw that they were fast asleep. Then he made his way to the other bedroom. His daughters, four-year-old Leah and six-year-old Magda, were playing house with their dolls. Both looked so much like their mother that he experienced a sharp pain in the center of his chest, which made it difficult for him to breathe. His oldest child had been named after her maternal grandmother, Anna's mother. Magdalene. He and Anna called her Little Magdalene while her mother was alive. Since her death, they had dropped the *Little* and given her the nickname Magda. His second daughter had been named Leah, after Joshua's grandmother who died before she was born.

As if finally sensing their father, both girls looked up. "*Dat*," Magda murmured. "Why aren't you resting? You shouldn't be walking around so much."

"I wanted to see you," he said with a fond smile.

"Vadder? Can we have a snack?" Leah looked at him with hope.

"*Ja*. Put your dolls on your bed and I'll find something for you to eat." Joshua turned to make his way carefully and slowly back to the kitchen. He'd opened the refrigerator and pulled out a carton of milk when Magda entered the room with Leah following a moment later. "Have a seat at the table."

Leah obeyed while her older sister remained standing. "*Dat*, can I help you with something?" Magda asked.

He eyed her with affection. "Milk and oatmeal cookies?"

His daughter grinned. "*Ja*. I'll get the cups." She pulled a stool over to the counter and used it to reach into a top cabinet. "Will you have milk, too?" she asked as she handed him two cups.

He had finished his coffee, and milk always went well with cookies. "*Ja*." He watched her stretch to reach for one more cup. "Please be careful." Joshua feared she would fall, and he wouldn't be able to get to her quick enough to ensure she was all right. He desperately needed to recover so he could take better care of her and his other children.

She bobbed her head. "*Okey*."

Joshua gave each of his daughters a cup of milk and

placed two of his sister's homemade oatmeal raisin cookies on paper plates for the three of them. He was pulling out a chair for himself when he heard a whimper from the twins' bedroom followed by crying. "Eat your milk and cookies. I need to check on your *bruders*."

To his surprise, Magda got up from the table. "I'll come with you. You need to be careful, Dat. I can help you, so you don't fall." She sounded so grown up at six years old. That his young daughter had taken on so much responsibility since her mother's death saddened him. She should be having fun being a child, not worrying about her sister and brothers…and him. "*Endie* Fannie told me to watch out for you, but she didn't have to. I can tell when you're hurting."

"I can use your help," he admitted with a small smile. His eldest was observant and wise beyond her years, and he was grateful for her.

His twin sons were awake and standing in their cribs with tears running down their little cheeks that stopped when they saw him. Seeing how tall they were as they stood made him realize that he would need to convert the cribs into toddler beds sooner rather than later. Magda put down the side of Jacob's crib and reached for her little brother. Joshua managed to do the same with JJ and set him on his feet.

"*Dat*, can they have cookies and milk, too?" his daughter asked.

"*Ja,* they can have some." Joshua watched as his eldest took each one's hand. He loved and appreciated all his children, but Magda stepped up whenever she thought he needed assistance. *She shouldn't need to worry about us.*

His daughter helped the twins into their high chairs before she retrieved the cookie tin from the counter and brought it to the table. Watching them, he felt sorrow that his sons wouldn't know or remember their mother.

Leaning heavily on his walker with his left hand, Joshua grabbed two sippy cups from the cabinet then filled both with milk for his sons. He handed one to each boy before he took a seat. After withdrawing two cookies from the tin, he placed one on each high chair tray.

"When will *Endie* Fannie come back?" Leah asked.

He took a sip of milk and then bit into a cookie. "I'm sure she'll stop by tomorrow."

They finished the snacks and went into the living room. Joshua took a seat in his favorite chair while his daughters kept their baby brothers busy.

A series of quick knocks reverberated from the kitchen. "I'll get it." Magda raced out of the room to get the door. Joshua followed her in time to see her open the door a crack and peek out to see who it was. He was proud of her for being cautious. "*Ja?*"

"You must be one of Joshua's *dechters*," he heard a woman's voice say with warmth. "The oldest. Magda?"

"Who are you?" his daughter asked without opening the door further.

"I'm Esther, a friend of your *endie* Fannie." There was a moment of silence. "I brought food."

Magda faced him. "Dat?"

He nodded. "You can let her in."

"Come in." His eldest stepped back after opening the door wider.

Joshua got a glimpse of the young woman as she came inside and turned to shut the door behind her. She wore a tab dress in pink with a white apron and head covering. Her smile reached her bright green eyes.

"What did you bring us?" Magda asked, eyeing the zippered item in Esther's hand.

Esther met his gaze and quickly looked away. "I've brought food for your lunch. Are you hungry?"

"We just had milk and oatmeal cookies, but they were a snack to hold us over." His daughter paused. "Can I see?"

The woman grinned. "*Ja,* of course you can." She came to the table and set down the odd-shaped cloth bag. "*Hallo,* Joshua." She met his gaze briefly with a small smile before she unzipped it.

"Esther. You didn't have to go to all this trouble." But he knew Fannie would have come if her friend hadn't, and in a way he was glad his sister had stayed at the Kings' house to enjoy herself with her husband and other family and friends.

"It's no trouble. We have so much food at the *haus.* It's a relief to have someone eat it." She took in his other children. "You must be Leah." Esther smiled at his youngest daughter.

Leah bobbed her head. "What kind of food did you bring?"

"Roast beef, potato salad and sweet-and-sour green beans. I also brought brownies, lemon bars and whoopie pies." Joshua saw Esther's attention center on his sons. "Which one is JJ and which one is Jacob?" she asked.

Magda pointed toward the twin on the right. "That's JJ."

Joshua saw Esther nod before she searched the contents of her bag. "Let's see what else we have in here."

Joshua Miller made her nervous, although she wasn't sure why. Was it because she knew she'd never have a husband and children—and he represented both? Conscious of his focused gaze, Esther shifted uncomfortably as she pulled food out of her large cooler bag. A plastic container of roast beef. A glass bowl with a lid filled with potato salad, and another one of the cold sweet-and-sour green beans with bacon. She extracted a small bowl of softened butter last. "I'll fetch the desserts from my buggy and be right back."

To her surprise, Magda followed her out into the yard. Esther reached toward the back bench seat to pick up the wrapped loaf of fresh bread, detecting the rich scent of yeasty goodness. "I baked this yesterday," she told the young girl as she handed it to her. Magda looked pleased as she accepted it. Joshua's eldest child was adorable in her light blue tab dress. Her light brown hair was rolled up neatly and pinned, but without a head covering.

Esther picked up the paper bag with the sweet treats, smiled at Magda then followed her back into the house.

"Dat, look! Fresh bread!" Magda grinned as she held up the loaf.

"There's butter in the small bowl." She set the paper bag on the kitchen counter and took out the desserts, then placed them in the corner. "For later," she explained when she turned and caught Joshua watching her. "Are you hungry enough to eat?"

"I am," both of his girls said in unison.

"Me!" Jacob banged on his high chair tray.

"Me! Me!" JJ cried as he followed his twin brother's lead.

Esther grinned as she looked from one child to another. They resembled tiny adults. All of them were precious in their Amish clothing—the boys with dark blue shirts with small suspenders and navy blue pants, the girls in their tab dresses, one light blue and the other purple. The boys had dark hair like their father while the girls' hair was a much lighter brown, with streaks of blond and a hint of red.

Her good humor disappeared when she met Joshua's stare. He wore a spring green shirt with black suspenders holding up navy blue triblend denim pants. Conscious of how handsome he was, she averted her gaze and spun around to get dishes from the cabinets, then proceeded to put a little bit of each food onto plates for the children. After debating whether she should prepare the meal for Joshua, she added bigger portions to a larger plate for him. She handed it to him. "What would you like to drink?" she asked the children.

"Milk." Magda got up and pulled a milk carton from the refrigerator. She brought it to the table then poured milk into all her siblings' glasses as well as hers. "Dat?"

Joshua pushed back his chair. "I'll make coffee."

"*Nay,* stay," Esther urged him. "I'll do it for you."

He opened his mouth as if to object, but then closed it. With a strange look in her direction, he stayed where he was.

She quickly made coffee, and when it was done, she poured him a cup. "Milk and sugar?" she asked, feeling self-conscious as she detected his clean, masculine scent—his soap and no doubt his shampoo.

"Both." He locked gazes with her, and she saw his brown eyes warm before she turned to get what he needed.

She set the coffee fixings before him and then checked to make sure that the children were eating. Esther then packed the rest of the food she had brought in plastic containers she'd found in a cabinet and stored them in the refrigerator for them to enjoy later.

"Are you going to eat with us?" Leah asked as she forked

a small piece of roast beef. Her eyes widened as she chewed and swallowed. "This is *gut*."

Esther grinned. "I'm glad you like it. And *nay*. I promised to eat with my *eldre*." She checked to see if the littlest Millers had enough food on their trays and that the pieces were small enough for them to eat. "I'll leave the desserts on the counter." She addressed Magda. "Will you be able to reach them?" To make sure the young girl could, she moved them closer to the edge but still safe from the little ones' reach. Once they'd finished their dinner, she collected the plates and utensils and put them in a dish basin, which she filled with soap and water.

"I'll be back in the morning to do the dishes." She didn't want to do them on a Sunday, and she would be back here cleaning the house the next day anyway.

"How do you know *Endie* Fannie?" Magda asked as Esther collected the empty food containers and placed them in her bag.

Esther picked up the bag in readiness to leave. "I work for her at her restaurant."

"*Ach*." Joshua's oldest daughter appeared puzzled. "Why will you be back tomorrow? I can wash dishes if you have something else to do."

"I'll be cleaning *haus* for you and your *dat* twice a week for a while until he feels better." Sensing the man's stare, she met Joshua's gaze. He didn't look happy but there was something else in his brown eyes that she couldn't read. "Do you need me to do anything for you before I leave?"

"*Nay*," he murmured. "I don't need you to do anything at all for me."

Esther experienced a burning sensation in her chest and in the pit of her stomach. He didn't want her here, she reminded herself. But she would show up anyway. Joshua was lucky enough to have children, young ones who needed him more than ever now. He needed to rest and recover so that he could be there for them, and the last thing he needed was to overdo it. The man would have to accept her assistance whether he liked it or not.

Chapter Four

❧

Esther knocked gently on Joshua Miller's back door with a breakfast casserole in her hand and waited. It was a cold Monday morning. The sun was bright, but it did little to heat up the air. It was the last week of October, but until today the weather had been unseasonably warm at fifty-five degrees or higher. Today, however, the temperature had dropped fifteen degrees to a chilly forty.

Within seconds, the door opened a tiny crack and Esther caught sight of a little girl's eyes in the opening. She could tell who it was by the child's height. "Leah," she greeted her with warmth. "It's Esther. I'm here to clean your *haus*. Would you please let your *dat* know I've arrived?" Holding up the large metal pan, she smiled. "I brought breakfast, too. Do you like sausage casserole?"

The door opened a little wider and she saw Leah bobbing her head.

"*Gut*. I'll wait here until you find out if it's safe to let me in, *ja*?" Esther remained where she was as the child ran off, calling for her *dat*.

Within seconds, Magda appeared in the open doorway and grinned. "Esther, come in. *Dat* is in the living room with his feet up." She stepped back to allow her entry. The girl's gaze lowered to the container in Esther's arms. "I heard you brought food."

Esther entered. "*Ja.* A sausage breakfast casserole." She set the cold metal pan on the counter then removed her coat and hung it on a wall hook before facing the child. "Do you like sausage?"

With a twinkle in her eye, Magda smirked. "Am I not Jonas Miller's granddaughter?"

Esther laughed. "You most certainly are, as it's your *grossdaddi*'s favorite."

She saw that the kitchen was empty. Esther turned on the oven to preheat. The dirty dishes were still in the sink, and she was glad Joshua had listened and left them. It also gave her something to do until breakfast was ready for the family. She washed the dishes quickly, pleased when Magda grabbed a dish towel and carefully dried each plate before setting them on the counter. "Is it this cold in the living room?" she asked.

Magda nodded. "Yes, but we are staying warm under blankets. Dad worked to get the fire going but I told him not to." She looked worried. "I think he had a rough night."

Esther felt concern for the injured man. "Once I get the casserole into the oven and put the coffee on for your *dat*," Esther said as she put away the dishes, "I'll check the woodstove." She took the lid off the metal pan filled with breakfast.

Joshua's daughter smiled. "*Danki*, Esther."

"You're most *willkomm*, Magda." The oven finished preheating, warming the kitchen quickly. Esther placed the casserole inside to reheat it. While the coffee perked, she followed the child into the living room where her siblings huddled under a quilt on the sofa. Her gaze settled on Joshua, who had his eyes closed as he rested his head on the back of an upholstered chair with his feet on an otto-man. Another quilt covered him from his chest to his feet.

Esther moved to the living room's woodstove and Joshua opened his eyes, locked gazes with her and frowned. "Esther."

"I told you I would be back today," she said pleasantly. "I've put a sausage casserole to heat for your breakfast. I'm going to get this woodstove going to take the chill from the *haus*." She smiled, hoping to soften his expression. "I won't be long. A big difference in temperature outside from yesterday, *ja*?"

He simply stared at her without replying until Magda drew his attention. "The casserole looks *gut*, *Dat*. It's sausage, just what our *grossvadder* likes."

Joshua's frown disappeared as he gazed at his daughter. The affection in his eyes for his children affected Esther greatly. It was clear the man loved them. She held back a sigh. If only he would accept her help as a friend.

She added kindling to the woodstove and waited for the fire to reignite before she added one log and then another. Soon, heat filtered into the room, warming it. "I put a pot of coffee on," Esther said. "Would you like your breakfast in here?"

"We can eat in the kitchen." Joshua pushed the quilt off his legs and reached for his walker. He was dressed in a light blue shirt and navy blue triblend pants held up by black suspenders. He wore sneakers that were necessary to help him walk. Esther stared at him a moment, taken by how good-looking he was.

Averting her gaze, Esther picked up both twins, one in each arm, and headed to the kitchen. She sat them in their high chairs without an issue, noting that the toddlers were dressed like their father. Then she smiled at their older sisters as they entered and took their seats at the table. Joshua maneuvered himself slowly into the room. She didn't wait for him to sit as she went to the stove to pour him a cup of coffee, the rich scent of it filling the air. She had a feeling that the man's struggle with his leg bothered him and made him regard himself as weak. She wasn't going to stare and make him feel worse. He probably felt bad enough struggling with the fire that morning without making him aware that she knew.

She set the coffee before Joshua after adding sugar and milk the way he liked, as she'd noted previously. Then, using the potholders she'd brought, she pulled the steaming casserole from the oven and set it carefully on a hot mat on the counter next to the stove.

"That smells delicious," Magda exclaimed, drawing Esther's attention. Today, she and Leah were dressed alike in light green tab dresses without head coverings since they were young and at home.

Esther grinned. "It's one of your *Endie* Fannie's favorite recipes." She cut the casserole into generous squares, then nodded at Magda when the young girl came to stand beside her as if she wanted to help. "What would you and your siblings like to drink? Milk?"

Magda nodded. "*Ja.* I'll get it." As Esther took down glasses for the children and plates for everyone, Joshua's oldest daughter got the milk from the refrigerator.

Esther set a piece on each plate with two pieces for Joshua on his. With a fork resting on each dish, she brought breakfast to the table. "Does anyone need anything? Ketchup?"

"No, *danki*," Joshua said, cutting into the hot casserole with his fork. "I appreciate this."

"It was no trouble," she assured him with a smile. Her good humor faded when the man stopped eating to gaze at her with a long look that told her he was confused, irritated and possibly grateful, which seemed to be the main cause of his discomfort.

Esther glanced away. "I'm going to take a look at the rooms to see if they need cleaning."

"They do," Magda said quickly. "I didn't have a chance to pick up after everyone."

She felt bad for the little girl who was trying to step into her late mother's shoes by caring for her siblings and helping around the house. "Not to worry. I don't mind doing it, and it won't take me long to make sure everything is clean and in its place. I'll be right back. My cleaning supplies are in my buggy." Esther donned her coat and left the house to get everything she needed from her buggy's back seat.

When she returned inside, the children had finished eating and left the room. Joshua was almost done with his breakfast. She placed her bucket with the cleaning supplies, mop and brooms in the corner of the kitchen near the refrigerator. "Can I get you anything else?" Esther asked, facing him.

"This is plenty," he said, his deep voice rippling down her spine. He seemed to hesitate. "*Danki* again."

"I'll get right to work then." She grabbed the tools of her trade and headed toward the bedrooms beyond the living room.

Magda stood as Esther walked through. "Can I help?" the girl asked.

She smiled at the child. "It would be great if you could keep an eye on your *bruders* and *schweschter*."

"*Okey.*" Magda made sure the twins were comfortable on the sofa with Leah before she sat on the floor near them.

"It's warmed up in here," Esther commented.

"*Ja.* It feels *gut.*" Magda appeared sad, probably thinking about the changes in their lives since her mother's death.

"Are you *oll recht*?" she whispered to the young girl.

The child nodded. "I'm well."

Esther didn't immediately move. "Would you like me to make sandwiches before I leave? I'll put them in the refrigerator so that you can take them out when it's lunchtime."

"Peanut butter and jelly?" Magda asked.

"Is that what you want or is that all you have?" She eyed the child with sympathy when Magda looked away as if embarrassed. "How about later I bring you some sandwiches?"

"I don't know if *Dat* will like that." Magda clearly wanted the lunch but didn't believe her father would approve.

"I understand." Esther smiled. "I'd better get to work. I'll start with the twins' room." The child stood as if to follow her. "Why don't you stay to keep your family company?" she suggested. "It looks like Leah wants to work on a puzzle with you."

Magda nodded. Esther saw the girl smile at her younger sister as she sat down beside her. Leah looked pleased when Magda started to help her take the puzzle pieces from a box.

The twins' room appeared clean but a little messy. Esther picked up a few toys and then folded the quilts before hanging one over the end of each crib. She did a quick dusting of the furniture followed by a hasty mop of the vinyl floor before heading to Magda and Leah's room. There she used her cell phone, which she'd tucked in a special pocket she'd sewn beneath the waistband of her apron when she had her business, to dial her employer and friend. "Fannie," she said. "I'm at your *bruder*'s. I brought a sausage casserole for him and the children."

"I know." Fannie sighed. "I found the money you left. You didn't have to pay for the casserole, Esther."

"I took it without asking," Esther said, "and so I paid for it." She paused. "I have a favor to ask. Would you have time to make sandwiches to bring to your *bruder*'s later for lunch? I thought to do it myself, but I don't think Joshua would appreciate it. I know he'll accept whatever you bring—and you probably know what he and the children like."

"I'll be happy to. Knowing my *bruder,* I understand well what you mean." Fannie must have covered her cell phone, as her voice became muffled as she spoke with a customer or an employee. She came back on loud and clear. "Sorry," she said. "I'll make lunch and take it to them." She paused. "Thanks for thinking of them, Esther. I appreciate it."

"I'm happy to do what I can for your family, and that includes Joshua and his *kinner.*"

Joshua's house was small compared to the ones she used to clean when she had her business. It didn't take her long to make her way through the bedrooms. When she got to the living room, Joshua had left the kitchen and joined his children there. She didn't want to do the room while the family was gathered there. She'd do it first the next time she came back to work.

"I'm all done except for this room and the kitchen. I'll do the kitchen now then take care of the living room during my next visit on Thursday," Esther said. She was happy to see all of them together resting comfortably, the way she'd found them when she first arrived. "I'll put the leftover casserole in the refrigerator. It will keep for a few days. I can reheat it for you the next time I come."

Joshua studied the woman who had brought breakfast and cleaned his house. She was more than pretty, with her unusual green eyes and her dark blond hair tucked under her *kapp*. The color of her dress beneath her white apron was a light shade of purple, which somehow highlighted her fair skin and lovely features. Her smile was radiant for his children whenever she talked with them, although it was more reserved for him.

Joshua wasn't sure what to make of her. She'd been kind enough to bring them two meals since he'd moved in, and she did a wonderful job cleaning his house. But he wasn't used to having a woman in his residence, not since Anna's passing. And he didn't like having a woman other than Anna in his home. It felt wrong, like a betrayal of his late wife's memory. But on the days Esther came, her help made it easier for his children to remain at home with him rather than at his father's house with his stepmother.

He wondered about Esther's life. Joshua knew that she worked at his sister Fannie's restaurant. She knew how to keep house well since she did such a good job with his. His father had told him that she used to have a cleaning business. Why did she stop? And why did she agree to work here?

Esther had gone to the kitchen, and his eldest daughter followed her. A short time later, the woman returned, went to the sofa and picked up the twins, one in each arm, without a word. His sons babbled as she started toward the rear of the house. She laughed at something JJ said and grinned as Jacob mimicked him.

He frowned. "Esther."

She stopped, and her good humor seemed to fade as she faced him. "*Ja?*"

"What are you doing?" he asked, curious that she hadn't immediately explained why she'd picked up his sons and walked off with them.

The woman turned to face him. "Getting the twins ready for their nap."

"I could have put them down in their cribs," he insisted.

"I'm not only laying them down to sleep, Joshua." She shifted Jacob in her right arm and wrinkled her nose as if she'd smelled something bad.

Magda approached him. "Dat, she's going to change their diapers first."

He caught and held Esther's gaze. "*Ach. Danki*," he said softly with a feeling of gratitude for her quick action. If not for his bad leg, he could have done the work to prepare them for naptime. It bothered him that he didn't feel fit enough to do everything, which frustrated him to no end. Did he have the right to keep his children at home with him during the day when his father and Alta enjoyed having them and could take better care of them? Yet he wanted them, needed them, here in the house with him. He loved them. They were the reason he had kept going since the death of their mother.

Esther stared at him a moment before a small smile curved her pink lips. "It won't take but a moment." Then she turned with his babies and headed toward their room.

"Go see if you can help her, Magda," he urged her after he saw his daughter's concern. "It's not easy dealing with twin little ones. You can watch one while she changes the other one. *Ja?*"

Magda nodded. She started to leave then paused. "Dat? I'm sorry I can't change both at the same time."

He felt a swell of love for his brave, sweet little girl. "Magda." She faced him. "You shouldn't have to worry about taking care of them. They are my *kinner*. I'm sorry it's taking so long for me to get well."

Tears filled the girl's eyes. "I want to help."

"Magda, you have…more than you realize. Now check on Esther and your *bruders*. She may be already done diapering them." Joshua wondered if the twins should be potty-trained by now. Anna would have taken care of that if she hadn't died. *Killed in a car accident that was my fault.*

He knew his girls hadn't taken long to train, but he didn't know about his boys. His *dat* knew a lot about raising children, having had five of his own. Maybe he'd ask him.

His father and siblings wouldn't agree that he was responsible for Anna's death since he'd done what the doctor had recommended. After the birth of the twins, Anna should never have been able to conceive again. If they had never gone, Anna might still be alive and his children would still have a mother to love. Or maybe not, since Anna giving birth again had been deemed unsafe by both doctors.

Joshua suddenly grabbed his walker, which was resting close to his chair, and struggled to his feet. He carefully made his way to the twins' bedroom until he reached the open doorway to watch Esther talk softly to each of his sons. Magda stood at her side as if captivated. Jacob and JJ gazed up at Esther as if she were someone special. And she was.

His six-year-old turned as if sensing his presence. Filled with affection for her, he smiled. "I better get back to Leah and the puzzle we started," she said. He saw Esther's nod before his daughter left the room.

Joshua observed as the woman took extra care to cover each of his sons with the quilts she'd made before reaching to run loving fingers through the hair of first one child and then his brother. She wished them a restful sleep and turned around, her gaze soft. Then she caught sight of him and stilled immediately. He saw her blink rapidly before shock entered her expression. "I'm sorry. I didn't realize you were there."

He gave her a warm, genuine smile. "I wanted to see them before they fell asleep. I'm sorry I'm not much help with this walker."

As if recognizing his voice, his son Jacob climbed to his feet and grinned at him. JJ followed his brother's example and did the same. "*Dat*," both cried. "*Dat, Dat!*"

His expression softened and he flashed a grin at Esther before he maneuvered his way toward the cribs. "You sleep now, little ones." Setting his walker to his side, he reached out to stroke Jacob's cheek before he lay the boy down. "Night, night, soohn." He did the same with JJ. "Sleep tight, soohn." Then he addressed them both. "I'll see you later. I'll be here when you wake up."

Joshua grabbed his walker, then turned around carefully to leave the room and was taken aback by the look on Esther's face. He thought he caught a glimpse of sadness in her pretty eyes. But then her expression changed as she smiled, pleased, which made him wonder if he'd imagined it.

She spun around and exited the room, and he slowly followed her. Esther stopped in the living room and waited for him to sit down. "Do you need anything else?"

"*Nay*, but I appreciate you asking." He settled more comfortably in his chair and lifted his hurt leg and then his good one onto the matching ottoman.

"I'll add a log to the fire, so the *haus* will stay warm," she said. "I have no idea how cold it will get this afternoon so I'll bring in extra wood for you. I'll turn off the oven before I leave. I think you'll be fine with the fire in here for a while."

Studying her from beneath lowered eyelids, he nodded. Joshua was amazed by her generous nature. She'd gone beyond her cleaning duties to ensure his comfort. He watched her place two logs onto the fire and bank it so that the flame and accompanying heat would last.

When she was done, she straightened then moved toward his daughters who, done with the puzzle, now sat on the sofa. Esther covered them with quilts, tucking one around each girl. "All snug," she murmured with a grin.

"*Danki,* Esther," he murmured, grateful for her kindness.

She left and returned moments later with an armful of wood. "That should help." She smiled. "Have a good day, Joshua. Fannie mentioned that she'll be stopping by later." She looked around the room as if to see if anything was out of place. "I'll see you in a couple of days."

Then Esther King returned to the kitchen, and he heard her move dishes around before the sound of the back door closing alerted him that she'd left. He fought the urge to watch her drive away, but he didn't give in to it. The realization that he was disappointed that she'd left bothered him.

Fifteen minutes after leaving Joshua's, Esther entered Fannie's Luncheonette through the back door. "*Hallo!*"

Fannie poked her head through the kitchen doorway. "Esther! How did you make out this morning?"

"Well." She entered the kitchen and hung up her coat with her bonnet. She then tied on a cooking apron. "While they ate breakfast, I cleaned the bedrooms and put the twins down for their naps. Before I left, I made sure there was enough fuel for the woodstove." Recalling Joshua's visit to his sons before they fell asleep, she smiled. "His *kinner* are *wunderbor.* Magda is sweet and helpful. Leah is well-behaved and follows Magda's guidance. And the boys— they are adorable and easy to please."

"*Ja,* Joshua and their *mudder* did a *gut* job raising them."

A glimmer of sorrow entered Fannie's blue eyes. "They are so young to have lost their *mam*." She sighed heavily. "I wasn't a youngster, but losing my *mam* was still difficult. My nieces remember her. The twins are young enough that they'll accept whoever Joshua weds someday."

Esther felt a little pang inside. "Do you think he will? Marry again?"

"With four *kinner*, he'll need to." Fannie put another egg casserole in the oven. It was still early enough to have customers coming in for breakfast. "Maybe he won't take a wife anytime soon, but although we are here to help him and his little ones, I think he will have to think about marriage eventually."

"What happened to her?"

Sadness filled Fannie's expression. "About eight months ago, Anna got pregnant again, too soon after a difficult time giving birth to the twins. Joshua was worried about her and insisted that she see a physician specializing in high-risk pregnancies, especially after her obstetrician recommended it. The visit went well, but on the way home, their hired car was hit by a drunk driver. Anna was killed instantly. Joshua was injured, with his legs suffering the worst. He's still grieving and blames himself for his wife's death since he insisted she see the specialist."

"He does?" Esther was shocked to hear this. "Even though her obstetrician agreed she should go?" She felt compassion for everything the man had suffered. What a shame that Joshua felt that way.

"*Ja.*" Fannie rubbed her forehead with the back of her hand. "It's tragic what he and the children have gone through."

Usually, people didn't say the name of a deceased loved one. But Esther knew that Fannie trusted her enough to explain why Joshua seemed closed off with her, a stranger in his house. *But not with his children*, she thought. *With them, he is loving and affectionate.*

"I'm sorry they've endured so much suffering." Esther sent up a silent prayer that Joshua and his family would heal.

Now that she knew his heart-wrenching story, Esther was more determined to help him. It didn't matter if he wasn't happy to see her. She would show up and do whatever she could for him and his family.

"I'll make the sandwiches for Joshua and my nieces and nephews. I thought I could take them over but I recently received a voicemail about a catering job. I need to call back an English couple we did a job for last summer. They want to host a Christmas party sometime in late November or early December—they weren't specific about the date in the message. What I do know is that they pay well. Would you be able to bring lunch to my *bruder*'s for me?" Fannie pleaded with a hopeful look in her blue eyes. "*Sighsogude?*" Please?

Esther hid her dismay. She doubted the man would be happy to see her again so soon.

Fannie bent to check the casserole in the oven and then straightened. "I'm sending a dessert, too. Joshua's favorite—triple chocolate cake."

"Then I'll take them lunch. But I told them you would stop by. I hope everyone's not upset when I show up instead of their *endie* Fannie." Esther brushed back a lock of hair that had escaped from beneath her *kapp*. "Your *bruder* won't be happy to see me back at the *haus*."

"He'll be fine. I'll write a short note explaining why I couldn't come myself." Using her hands, Fannie mixed the ingredients in her bowl to form bread dough. "Usually when I stop by, I'm there to pick up his children. Joshua hates when we insist that his *kinner* should be with us so that he can rest."

"I understand how he must feel." Esther started to grate a block of cheddar cheese to be used in future casseroles. "He loves them. You can see it in his expression whenever he looks at them." She could feel Fannie staring at her. She gazed back. "What?"

Her friend and employer smiled. "I...you seem to know my *bruder* well."

"I don't." Esther averted her eyes as she blushed. "I'm just observant."

Fannie dumped the bread dough onto a floured bread-board and began to knead it. "I'm glad you agreed to take on his *haus*, Esther. I don't like the thought of him struggling to do everything on his own. I'm afraid he'll fall and injure himself further."

"Anyone would be happy to help," Esther said, feeling humble.

"*Nay*, you're wrong. Not everyone would step in like you have," Fannie insisted. "You're a *wunderbor* friend who is always ready to lend a hand."

What Fannie had implied bothered Esther. She was naturally an observant person, wasn't she? It couldn't possibly be because her senses seemed to sharpen, making her notice every little thing about Joshua whenever he was near. Or could it?

Two hours later, Esther was at Joshua Miller's with a box of sandwiches and a bag of canned drinks. She set down the bag and knocked. Moments later, Joshua stood at the open door, leaning on his walker, and scowled at her. "What are you doing here?"

Esther picked up the bag and held it out with the box. "Your *schweschter* made you lunch. She can't get away from the luncheonette, as someone wants to hire her for a catering job. She asked me to bring the food for her."

"Come in," he said grumpily. He fumbled backward away from the door.

With a sigh of resignation, she entered the house and locked gazes with the man who now struggled to sit in a kitchen chair. Turning from him, Esther set everything on the kitchen counter and heard the children as they talked and laughed in the living room.

"Did Fannie really send this, or is this your doing?" he asked irritably.

She glared at him. "Does it matter?" Esther was sick and tired of his attitude.

He scowled. "I can't help but wonder why you show up so often."

"Fannie sent the food, so eat or not. I don't care."

Esther opened the box that held lunch and extracted Fannie's note, which she silently handed him. There were also paper plates inside.

"What's this?" Joshua growled as he took the paper.

"Read it." Esther pulled out sandwiches and put each on a paper plate, then brought them to the table. Fannie had let her know which sandwich her brother and each child liked, so she knew which lunch went before each seat and high chair tray. The bag of drinks included juice and iced tea. He didn't say another word as she set up lunch for him and his children. Then, without asking for permission, she went into the living room to get his four youngsters.

"Esther!" Magda cried with delight, jumping to her feet. "You're back."

She managed a smile. "I brought lunch. Everything is on the table."

Leah grinned at her as she scrambled to follow her.

She reached down to take the hand of each twin. "Come, little ones. Are you hungry?"

"Want to eat," Jacob said.

"Me, too!" JJ smacked his lips eagerly.

Esther fought the urge to ruffle their dark hair with her fingers. Although they were identical, she found it easy to tell each boy apart. There was a slight difference in their faces, but not everyone would see it. She led them slowly into the kitchen.

The children were chatting and laughing, eager to dive into the food she'd had brought, compliments of their aunt. Esther made sure that they had their drinks and anything else they needed before she left.

"You're leaving?" Magda asked, looking sad.

Esther was glad that someone wanted her in the house, despite her father's attitude. "I must get back to work at Fannie's."

She left and hurried to her buggy. When she saw the cake on the back seat, she groaned. She forgot Fannie had sent dessert for them. Esther didn't want to go back inside, but she had to. There was no way she could explain to Fannie that she had refused to bring in the cake because she didn't want to encounter Joshua again.

As she approached the house, Esther dreaded her return after how rude he'd been. She raised her hand to knock when she heard crying inside. Concerned, she pushed open the door and saw Joshua sprawled on the floor. His children were in tears. Magda stood over him, looking worried.

"Esther!" Magda sobbed when she caught sight of her. "*Dat* fell!"

Chapter Five

❧

Joshua groaned inwardly. The last person he wanted to see him helpless was Esther. After his bad behavior had prompted her to leave, he'd gotten up from the table to go after her to apologize, but then he stumbled, knocked over his walker in his haste and fell forward. He hadn't meant to be rude and irritable, but he was frustrated with his condition. His lengthy recovery was getting to him, and he'd taken it out on her...a good, kind woman who had only wanted to help him and his family.

After managing to roll onto his back, he'd searched for something to grasp to pull himself up but found nothing.

Esther looked alarmed to find him on the floor. She put the cake on the counter and addressed Magda. "Take the children into the other room. I'll help your *dat*. *Okey*?"

With a relieved glance in his direction, Magda nodded and hustled the children into the living room.

When they were gone, Esther approached him.

"What are you doing back here?" he asked as he futilely fought to get to his feet.

"I forgot to bring in the cake your *schweschter* sent. It's triple chocolate. Fannie said it's your favorite." She eyed the chair where he'd been sitting, as if gauging how far she would have to move him to get him back in it. "What were you trying to do?" she asked pleasantly—more pleasantly than he deserved.

"I don't need your help." Joshua didn't want her assistance, but he knew that he had no choice.

She studied him calmly. "You are a stubborn man, Joshua Miller." She pulled the chair farther away from the table. "Whether you want me to or not, I'll be helping you up off this floor."

He blinked as he looked up at her. "You're bossy." Despite his current situation, he couldn't help being amused.

She didn't smile as she crouched and examined his legs with concern. "Are you hurt?"

"I'm fine."

She locked gazes with him. When he shifted his legs to ease a muscle cramp, he grimaced, and judging by the look on her face, she saw. Suddenly, she stood and pulled out her cell phone. "I'll call your *vadder* to help."

"*Nay!*" He closed his eyes, unwilling to explain but realizing that he must. "If you call him, he'll take the children away from me. He'll let Alta care for them during the day while I rest and recover before they bring them back at night. I'm afraid they'll want to keep them overnight as well. I want them—need them—here with me."

Joshua saw her expression soften. "I understand." He sighed with relief when she tucked her cell phone back into her apron. "We'll manage together." With a determined look on her face, she tugged the kitchen chair close to him. "It will be easier if we can get you onto this first, then you can use your walker to stand."

Esther got behind him and took hold of his waist. "I'll count to three and then I'll lift you into the right position." When he shot her a skeptical look, she grinned. "What? You don't think I can do it?"

Joshua didn't answer her question. "I'm ready if you are."

To his surprise, she laughed at his refusal to challenge her. *What an amazing woman*, he thought, pleased by the sound of her good humor. "Hold on," she instructed as she released him. "Don't try to move. I have an idea." She grabbed towels from a kitchen drawer and folded them to form a cushion for the chair seat. "Let's get you on your hands and knees first."

With her assistance, he was able to place his hands on the kitchen floor. He put down his right knee then groaned as his left touched the hard floor next, and she quickly held on and shifted him to make it easier for him.

"Are you *oll recht*?" she asked with concern, the sound of her voice soft in his ear.

He nodded. "I'm *okey*."

"We need to get you upright long enough to have you stand and turned around to sit, *ja*? On the count of three," she said, "push up onto your good leg and I'll support you as you rise." Noting his silent agreement, she counted. "One. Two. Three."

With her hands around his waist, Esther pulled him up. The chair started to tip, and she gasped until it righted itself as Joshua rose to his feet. He shifted until he stood on his good leg then spun around and sat down. As he lowered himself to the chair seat, she lost her connection with him and fell backward onto the floor.

Flat on her back, she met his stunned gaze and then she emitted a full-blown belly laugh. Joshua stared at her with wide eyes, wondering if she needed his help, but then she scrambled to her feet, her mirth loud in the kitchen.

Magda burst into the room with a worried expression. When she saw Esther standing beside his chair, his *dochter* looked relieved. Joshua grinned when he saw the woman's lips twitch, as if she was struggling to hide her amusement. "You can come for dessert in a few minutes," Esther said with a grin.

"*Okey,*" Magda said with a small smile before she left to rejoin her siblings.

Esther picked up the tipped-over walker from the floor and placed it within his reach. Joshua stood and balanced himself with it, and she quickly moved his chair back to the table, where he shifted to sit down again.

"What were you doing when you fell?" she asked softly.

Joshua stared at her. "I was coming after you."

She blinked, appearing startled. "Why?"

He drew in a sharp breath and released it. "To apologize. I'm sorry I was bad-mannered. I appreciate everything you do for us...for me...and I'd like you to stay." He watched her expression change. "To continue to clean, I mean," he hurriedly added.

Before Esther could respond, Magda reappeared, looking shy. "Can we come in?"

Esther smiled. "*Ja*, of course. Get your *schweschter* and *bruders*. It's time for cake!"

Joshua watched as she served everyone a piece of cake, and when his children were finished, she wiped and dried the twins' mouths using a damp tea towel. The girls used their napkins to clean around their lips.

"*Danki,* Esther," Magda murmured a short time later when everyone was done with the treat.

"My pleasure, little one." Esther picked up their dishes and moved them into the sink. "Would you take your brothers and sister into the living room while I speak with your *vadder*?"

Magda nodded. When Joshua's children had left, Esther pulled out a chair and sat next to him. "Are you *okey* or do you need to see a doctor?" Her green eyes regarded him with concern.

"I'm fine. My leg doesn't hurt much. But I've been thinking," he said with a sigh, "it's taking too long for me to recover. Maybe a doctor here in New Berne can help when the others didn't seem too concerned with my recovery time." He paused to take a calming breath. "I must be honest, though. It's possible they suggested something that I should do once I left the hospital." He'd been struggling to accept the horror of his wife's death. "I wasn't exactly in the right frame of mind to remember instructions I may have been given before I was discharged." He held her gaze. "I want to get well for my children. Please don't say anything to my family. As I told you, they'll insist on my *kinner* staying with them so that I can rest."

Esther nodded and stood. "I won't tell anyone. Just let me know if there is anything I can do."

Joshua looked relieved. "*Danki,* Esther."

"I need to get back to the luncheonette." She reached for her coat. "It's getting cold outside. I'll add wood to the stove before I go." She seemed surprised when he didn't object. "See you later in the week. *Ja?*"

Joshua pushed back his chair. "I appreciate your help."

She grinned. "Take care, Joshua." Then she left, looking pleased that she'd been able to assist to him.

"I appreciate you taking me to this doctor, Dat," Joshua said as he gazed at the man beside him in the buggy. He was grateful that his father had always been there for him and his siblings, and now his grandchildren.

His *dat* briefly met his gaze. "I was happy when you asked me to find a specialist for you to confer with, and that you were able to get an appointment so quickly. I know you've been feeling frustrated with your walker and slow recovery." His eyes on the road again, Jonas continued. "And Alta is excited to spend this time with our grandchildren."

"I know you liked having them at your *haus*, Dat, but I need them to be home with me." He loved his children with all his heart. They were all he had left of his beloved late wife. "The house is empty and cold without them."

His father put on his directional signal and turned right into the parking lot of a large medical building. He stopped near the hitching post meant for Amish buggies and met his gaze. "Soohn, I understand. Which is why I'm glad you're here. When you told me last week that you hoped a doctor in New Berne would be able to help you, I was thrilled." It was easy to see his *dat*'s sincerity. "Do you think it's easy for me to see you struggle? It's not. An adult or not, you are my child. I want only the best for you." He grinned and then got out of the buggy. Joshua waited while his parent tied up the horse. Then his father came to his side of the buggy where he took out a walker and unfolded it for Joshua's use. "With prayers and *gut* medical advice," his *dat* said, "I have a strong feeling that you'll be walking on your own soon."

They headed inside the building to the office where Joshua would be seeing the new doctor. When he was called into the back, he was glad that his father came in with him. A technician in the office came to take Joshua to get X-rays of both his legs. Afterward, he and his *dat* sat in the exam room, waiting for the doctor to check the films and advise them about the results.

Dr. Ramsey, his new orthopedist, entered moments later. "Let's see what we have," he said as he brought up the digital images on his computer screen. As he gazed at them, he frowned. "Your films look fine. Your leg is healed. I see where a surgeon inserted pins in it after the accident, which were surgically removed later. How did you make out with physical therapy?"

"I didn't go," Joshua said, surprised by the news. "I don't remember being prescribed any." He inhaled sharply. "I'd lost my wife and can't remember much of anything during that time except my loss."

The doctor nodded. "I understand." He checked on the X-rays again. "I believe we can get you back on your feet." He met Joshua's gaze. "First, I want you to ditch the walker and start using a cane. Then I'd like you to start physical therapy this week. I'll write you a prescription. You need to build back strength in your leg—both legs, since you've been on the walker for so long." He typed something into his computer. "I'll be right back."

True to his word, Dr. Ramsey returned and handed Joshua a sheet of paper with the prescription. "You can go where you want for PT, but I suggest using the practice here in this building. The therapists are excellent. If you'd like, I can have my nurse make an appointment for you."

Joshua looked at his father, who nodded. "Thank you, doctor. I'd appreciate that." He stared at the paper in his hands. "You believe I'll be able to walk again without a problem?"

"Absolutely," the physician said. "Your legs look good. Someone did a good job in setting your fracture. I'd like you to go to PT two or three times a week for the next three weeks then return here for a follow-up. Have my receptionist set up the appointment for you."

"All right." Joshua stood and grabbed his walker before he followed his doctor and father out of the exam room. He was hopeful. Using a cane would be more convenient than moving about with the walker. And he had one in his bedroom. Someone in his former church district in Illinois had given it to him, but he'd been afraid to stop using the walker without a doctor's approval. Now that he knew his left leg had healed as much as his right, it would be easier for him to use it.

During the drive home, Joshua felt pleased by his doctor's positive outlook, but he knew he had to do the work to get better.

His father glanced at him with a smile. "It was a *gut* appointment," his *dat* commented.

"*Ja*, it was." Joshua grinned.

"There is something I want to discuss with you." His parent kept his eyes on the road.

"What is it?"

"*Soohn*, you need to seriously consider taking a wife," his *dat* said carefully. "I know you are grieving, but your children need a *mudder*."

Pain lanced inside Joshua's chest. "Anna hasn't been gone that long."

"Your *kinner* can't wait until you feel ready to marry," his father insisted. "Think about it. We have a *wunderbor* matchmaker in New Berne. I can get her to come to the *haus*."

"*Nay*. Not yet." He had enough to think about for now with his physical therapy. "I need to walk again. Then I'll let you know." He'd rather find his bride on his own. Joshua knew he would never love again, and it didn't seem fair to marry someone without love, but he realized his dad was right. He had no choice if he wanted someone to care for and mother his children.

His *dat* met his gaze. "Joshua, it's been almost seven months now since you lost Anna. I know it doesn't seem long enough, but it's time."

Joshua scowled. He didn't like the idea at all. "You make it sound as if it will be easy."

"Marriage is never easy. I'm sure some woman will be happy to wed you and take care of your little ones. They need a *mam*'s touch, soohn." His father's gaze was on the road. "If you and your siblings had been younger when your *mam* died, I would have married again. It would have hurt, but I would have done it. I would do anything for all of you."

His *dat* had wed again, but it was a long time after his *mam*'s death. But his father was right, although it bothered Joshua to admit it, even to himself. He sighed. "I'll give it some serious thought." After all, he had four young children to think about, and he loved them enough to do whatever was needed for them to feel cherished and happy. Magda couldn't continue with the responsibilities she'd taken on of caring for Leah and the twins.

His little ones needed a mother, and he had to be willing to give them one. He wanted his oldest daughter to enjoy life as a child, and when the twins continued to grow as toddlers, they would become more active and harder to manage. A wife would help raise them, care for them and provide a woman's touch that had been lacking since Anna's death.

His father smiled. "That's all I ask."

With his face turned toward the side window, Joshua gazed at the passing scenery then closed his eyes as he tried to imagine ever feeling happy and at peace again. Marrying someone else would feel like a betrayal to his late wife.

Anna, I love and miss you. I'm sorry that you're gone. I know your doctor said you needed a specialist, but I should have figured something else out, found someone closer so we didn't have to travel so far.

I couldn't protect you. Please, please forgive me.

Chapter Six

It had been two weeks since Esther last cleaned Joshua's house. During that time, his children had been at Jonas's place while Joshua had consulted a doctor about his leg and started a three-week course of physical therapy. Fannie had told her that she didn't think he'd need his residence cleaned during that time. She'd told Esther she would stop by and check the house, but it hadn't appeared dirty.

"Do you think he still wants me to continue to clean for him?" Esther cracked eggs into a bowl for the restaurant's omelet special of the day.

"*Ja,* of course." Fannie grated a thick block of cheddar cheese. "Joshua is at physical therapy this morning. Today is a *gut* day for you to go back. I haven't been to look at it lately. You can use your key to get the work done before everyone comes home and gets in your way."

Esther agreed. "*Okey.* I'll head over there now." There was something about Joshua Miller that captured her attention like no other man. It seemed like forever since she'd seen him last. Was he making progress with his physical therapy? She prayed daily for his improvement. Once he was well and no longer needed her, she knew she'd see him and the children only on church service days and occasionally on Visiting Sundays. That prospect hurt her more than it should have. His father had hired her to do a job. She sighed, knowing that she was nothing more than Joshua's house cleaner.

Pushing away her sadness, she drove to Joshua's after a brief stop at home for a plate of brownies she'd made yesterday. While she wouldn't see the children or their father this morning, she could do something nice by leaving the family a snack for later.

Esther entered the residence, grateful to be out of the cold. She immediately appreciated the warmth inside. But the empty house seemed too quiet. She missed hearing the children giggling and laughing as they played. Magda, Leah and the twins were a joy to be around, and their father... well, he seemed larger-than-life whenever she was near him. She hadn't seen him since the day he'd fallen, when she'd helped him to his feet. Esther heard he was doing well and was glad for him, but she couldn't help wondering if he was upset because she'd seen him at his most vulnerable.

After hanging up her coat, she went to work in the kitchen, washing and drying a few dirty dishes and wiping the counters and table before checking inside the propane-powered refrigerator to see if the family had enough food. Esther then mopped the floor and went to work in the other rooms. Surprised by how spotless the house was for a family of five after two full weeks, she wondered if Joshua would need her anymore, whether he'd found someone else to do the job instead. It didn't take her long to run through the children's rooms. She changed the sheets on the girls' beds and the boys' crib mattresses.

There was a gas-powered washer in the bathroom. She added the sheets to the tub but didn't start it. She went into Joshua's bedroom next to see if she needed to change his bedding as well.

As soon as she stepped inside, Esther immediately detected a pleasing scent—a mixture of soap and something masculine that was all Joshua. She briefly closed her eyes and savored it with each inhale. To her surprise, the bed was made and his clothes picked up. She did a quick dusting of the furniture and swept the floor. Then she peered out his bedroom window to enjoy the view of the backyard. The sudden loud sound of a shutting door made her freeze.

"Fannie?" It was Joshua.

She inhaled sharply. He'd expected his sister. Grabbing her supplies, Esther hurried out of his bedroom. "It's just me."

They met in the living room. Joshua blinked with surprise to see her.

Esther was embarrassed to be caught in his house without his consent. "Fannie suggested I clean while you were gone so I don't disturb anyone."

He studied her closely with intense brown eyes. The man looked good. Physical therapy seemed to have worked wonders for him. He no longer used his walker. The cane that supported him made him stand upright. He appeared taller, more powerful and male.

"I have a few things left to do," she said, "and then I'll leave."

Esther hurried into the kitchen, aware of his presence as he followed her. "I don't think you need me here twice a week," she said. "I can come once a week or monthly if you prefer." She bit her lip. "If you still want me to clean for you." Without waiting for a reply, she picked up the plate of frosted brownies and handed it to him. "This is for you and the children." She shifted uncomfortably under Joshua's stare. Their fingers brushed as he accepted the plate from her, and she inhaled sharply at the touch. As he placed the brownies in the refrigerator, she took a quick moment to take a calming breath.

He straightened and then faced her. "*Danki.* The *kinner* will enjoy them."

She acknowledged his thanks with a brief nod. "You look well. It's nice to see you moving about more easily. I guess your fall didn't hurt your leg."

"Thankfully, it didn't," he said gruffly. "I learned the bones in both of my legs have mended well. I just need to get my muscles back to full strength. I've already seen a big improvement, probably because I had to put weight on my legs with the walker. Dr. Ramsey told me to only use the cane now." He gazed at her with an intensity that unsettled her. "It's helped."

"That's *gut.*" Esther swallowed hard. His continued scrutiny made her self-conscious. "I stripped the beds in the children's rooms then put on clean sheets. The dirty ones are in the washer," she said, talking fast as she turned away. "I just have to start the wash and then hang them to dry."

"No need for you to stay," he said. "I can handle it."

She caught a sudden strong whiff of his scent. Esther spun around and gasped as he stood within two feet of her. "I'm sorry. I'll go. I feel like I'm intruding. I know you don't want me here."

A sudden commotion at the back door heralded the arrival of Joshua's children. Jonas entered behind them. Esther smiled, pleased for the chance to see Joshua's little ones before she left.

"Esther!" Magda cried and ran to hug her.

Joshua watched, shocked, as his daughters wrapped their arms around Esther's waist while the woman grinned down at them, giving them her full attention. His father picked up the twins before they could rush Esther the way his little girls had.

"Did you have a nice time with your *grosseldre*?" Esther asked.

Magda bobbed her head. "*Ja*. We helped Grossmammi Alta make a cake." She shot her grandfather a look. "It was *gut*, wasn't it, Grossdaddi?"

"It was," Jonas said with affection. "Lemon cake with lemon frosting."

Esther smiled at his girls with a brightness in her expression that captured Joshua's attention.

"Down!" Jacob cried, struggling to get out of his grandfather's arms.

"Down," JJ mimicked.

His father set down the twins. Joshua watched, astounded, as the boys ran to Esther, lifting their arms to her, asking to be picked up. Releasing his daughters with a soft pat on their heads, she lifted the twins, one in each arm. Amazed at his children's comfort with her, Joshua could only stare. He met his *dat*'s gaze as he felt his father shift closer to him. With a jerk of his head, his *dat* gestured toward the young woman, who spoke animatedly with his daughters and sons. He could immediately read his father's thoughts by his look, recalling the conversation they'd had previously about him finding a wife. He was likely insinuating that Esther would make a good mother for his children and he should think seriously of marrying her.

"Is it *oll recht* if they each have a brownie?" she mouthed to him.

"*Ja*, it's fine." Joshua fixed his gaze on Esther, who urged his *kinner* to sit at the kitchen table. The young woman pulled the plate of brownies from the refrigerator and spoke to them with affection as she put the brownies on dishes, one for each child, and poured them glasses of milk. She looked up, and her smile fell when she caught him staring at her. "Would you like one?" she asked, looking shy. He shook his head.

Esther smiled uneasily. "I should go," she said. "You have my cell number."

"I'd like you to clean once a week," Joshua blurted out after she picked up her cleaning supplies and headed toward the door.

She froze and glanced back, her expression soft. "I can do that. Call me if you need me sooner."

"See you later, Esther!" Magda exclaimed before she took a bite of her brownie.

Then, with a genuine grin for his children and Jonas, she left, and Joshua wished he had enough strength in his legs to help carry her belongings to her buggy and have a private word with her.

As his children enjoyed their treats, Joshua turned to his *dat*, who smirked at him.

"*Nay*," he said quietly, for his parent's ears only. "I'm not ready, and when I am, I'll find myself a wife."

"I didn't say a word." His father regarded him with amusement.

"The look on your face is louder than any words." Joshua eyed his children and then faced his father again. "I know they need a *mudder*," he said quietly so only his *dat* could hear. "I'll do what I can to give them everything they need. But please, vadder, don't mention this to anyone. *Okey*?"

His father gave him a soft smile as he placed a hand on Joshua's shoulder. "You are a *gut* man, soohn. I'm glad to have you home again."

Joshua felt a wash of warmth and love for the man who had always been there for him and his siblings. His *dat* had suffered when his *mam* had passed on, but he'd never let his children down, not a single time. "I'm happy to be here."

Jonas smiled. "I need to get home. Alta will already be missing your little ones, and I promised to take her out for lunch."

"I appreciate everything you've done and continue to do for me, *dat*."

"I haven't done anything for you and your siblings that you wouldn't do for your little ones." His *dat* saw the cell phone that Fannie had given him. "*Gut!* I see you got the cell phone."

"*Ja.* I heard you paid for it." Joshua shook his head. "I'll give you the money for it."

"Why? You're my *soohn.* Why can't I do something nice for you? Besides, it's for my sake as well as yours. I like knowing you can call me if you need anything. It was Fannie's idea. I have one, too—thanks to your *schweschter.*" He grinned. "She kept pushing for me to get one, and she was right. I can contact anyone I'm concerned about or whenever there is an emergency." His father hesitated, looking thoughtful, as if he needed to find the right words for something important he wanted to say. "I forgot to tell you. Alta and I won't be able to watch our *kins kinner* next week while you're at physical therapy." A little smile curved his lips as a twinkle lit up his brown eyes. His voice lowered. "You may want to consider asking Esther to watch them."

Joshua eyed his parent with suspicion. "Are you really too busy, or are you trying to get Esther to spend more time with Magda, Leah and the twins?"

His *dat's* expression became serious. "We honestly won't be available. Alta's daughter Mary is pregnant with her second baby. She's not due until late spring, but Alta wants to go for a short visit. We'll leave on Monday but will be back in a couple of days."

Joshua felt instantly better about his father's suggestion to have Esther babysit for him. He offered him a smile. "I suppose I could give her a call and ask."

His father nodded. "I'll see you on Sunday for service, Joshua. We'll be happy to pick you up and help with your *kinner*."

"That would be *gut*, Dat." Joshua listened as his *dat* told him he'd be there to get them at eight on Sunday. After his father left, he joined his children at the kitchen table and snagged a brownie off the plate. He took a bite and hummed his appreciation for the moist chocolate goodness with rich chocolate frosting, which just might become his new favorite treat.

Esther stepped inside her mother's warm kitchen and noted the rich scent of roasting meat, which made her mouth water. "I'm sorry I wasn't here earlier to help with supper." She had stayed after the restaurant closed to prepare the breakfast and lunch specials for the following day.

Her mother smiled at her. "You had things to do, and I had plenty of help."

Linda briefly stopped peeling potatoes to wave at her. "It was steady at Fannie's this morning, but enough customers to handle them by myself."

Esther hung up her coat then faced Linda with a smile. "Schweschter, *danki* for filling in until I could get back from Joshua's."

Her sister grinned. "It was no problem. I'll cover for you whenever you need me." She picked up a knife and cut up the peeled potatoes into small chunks before she tossed them into a large stainless steel pot. "I'm sure it got busy after I left."

"It wasn't bad. It was easy enough for me and Hannah to manage the lunch crowd." Hannah Lapp, a cousin of Rachel King, had come to New Berne from Happiness to spend time with family. After the young woman had mentioned how much she liked it in their community, Fannie had offered her a job. Hannah had been happy to accept and admitted she was pleased to be able to stay and escape from under the watchful eyes of her older brothers. Hannah turned out to be a hard worker and a wonderful addition to their team.

"That's *gut*," her sister said as she removed a loaf of fresh bread from the oven and set it on a hot mat on the kitchen counter. "*Ach,* Jonas stopped by a short while ago. He invited our family to Thanksgiving dinner."

Her mother added water to the pot of potatoes before she set it on the stove and turned on the burner. "Fannie and her family will be there too. So will Joshua and his *kinner.*"

A frisson of warmth ran up her spine on hearing Joshua's name. The knowledge that she'd be enjoying Thanksgiving dinner with her family, the man and his little ones, as well as her aunt and uncle, gave her a rush of pleasure.

Esther pulled out the usual number of plates with utensils and set the table. "I assume everyone is home for supper."

"*Ja,* the boys are upstairs," Linda said as she stirred the potatoes.

"Do we want chowchow this evening?" Esther asked her mother after she added napkins to the place settings. The sweet-and-sour pickled vegetables from their garden's last offerings were delicious and simple to serve at supper.

Her *mam* smiled. "Why not?"

Esther nodded before she retrieved two quart-size canning jars from the pantry. With three hungry brothers, they would need both. She dumped the contents into a large serving bowl. Her cell phone rang as she set it on the table. With a frown, she pulled it from her apron. "*Hallo?*"

"Esther, this is Joshua Miller," the man's deep, pleasant voice greeted, startling her.

"*Ach, hallo,* Joshua," she replied as her heart started to race. "Do you need to cancel next week?" She managed to hide her disappointment.

"*Nay.* I have a favor to ask."

"*Okey.* Hold on a second." She realized that her mother and sister were listening closely as they studied her with curiosity. Esther shot them a look before she escaped into another room. "I'm back." She hesitated. "What do you need?" Her voice was soft, as she didn't want anyone to overhear.

"I'm sorry to bother you," he began.

"It's no bother," she insisted.

"*Ach, gut.*" His deep voice rippled down the nape of her neck. "I hate to ask you—"

"Whatever it is, it's fine, Joshua," Esther said. She would do whatever he needed, no matter what it was, even if it upset and bothered her. Because what if she got in too deep with him and his children? The family was still grieving over the loss of a wife and mother. Esther knew she should keep her distance from them since their future would never be hers. Since learning of her medical diagnosis, she'd had to accept that her path was now different, with a life that didn't include a family of her own.

"I have physical therapy for at least another week. Alta and my *vadder* can't watch my *kinner.* I was wondering if you would mind babysitting while I'm at my appointments, starting this Monday." She heard his quick inhalation of breath before he continued. "Alta wants to visit her *dochter.*

They'll be gone a few days." He paused. "It's possible they may return before my Friday session, but I'd appreciate it if you plan to watch my *kinner* on that day. If you can."

"I'll be happy to watch your little ones." Esther could barely control the sudden burst of happiness at the fact that Joshua had reached out for her help, that he trusted her with his children. "It will be a pleasure. I enjoy spending time with them. Let me know when you want me there."

"*Danki,* Esther." Had she imagined it or did his voice warm as he thanked her?

Joshua then gave her his schedule and the times she needed to be available for babysitting. After she assured him that she would be there, she hung up and returned to the kitchen.

Her mother met her gaze with raised eyebrows.

"Joshua Miller has physical therapy next week," she said calmly, although she could feel the thunder of her rapid heartbeat. "And Alta isn't available to watch his *kinner* so I agreed to babysit."

"That's *gut*. His little ones like you." The smile on her *mam's* face made her shift uncomfortably.

Esther frowned. "Who told you that?"

"Fannie told me at work," Linda said, jumping into the conversation.

Had her employer talked with her sister about her and Joshua's children? Esther wasn't sure how she felt about that.

Her brothers and father joined them a short while later, and the women put supper on the table. Esther managed to smile and tease her siblings, while silently assuring herself that she would be fine babysitting next week. At least, she hoped so. Even amid her family, she had trouble thinking of much of anything but her agreement to watch Joshua Miller's adorable children. On the days she'd be watching the children, she would have to see Joshua every day before he left and when he returned. The prospect made her heart race and her face flush. She knew she probably should have said no. But how could she when she loved spending time with Magda, Leah and the twins? Closing her eyes, Esther calmed herself by trying not to be overwhelmed about being there for the handsome man and his family when she'd never have a husband or children of her own.

Chapter Seven

Joshua helped his children into his father's buggy and then carefully slid in behind them. "*Danki* for taking us to service at Fannie's this morning."

"She's been looking forward to hosting our congregation," his *dat* said as he drove his buggy out of the driveway and onto the road. "And since you haven't been to visit her at home yet, she is eager to show you her *haus*."

"It will be nice to get a tour." Joshua looked forward to seeing where his sister and her husband, David, lived with their three-year-old daughter, Rose.

He studied his sister's house as his *dat* pulled onto the lane that led to a large two-story white residence, with five windows upstairs and two downstairs flanking the central door on the covered porch.

Two vehicles were parked in the yard—one near the barn and the other one close to the side door. His *dat* chose to park behind the one closest to the house. Joshua climbed out, leaned his cane against the buggy and assisted his elder two out of the buggy before he reached inside for the twins.

His father picked up Jacob and JJ while Alta carried her food offering for the day. Joshua grabbed his cane from the side of the buggy, and they started toward the house with his girls beside him. The door opened and Esther came out, bundled against the cold in a dark coat with a black bonnet. He watched as she leaned into the buggy then straightened with two foil-covered platters in her hands.

"Esther!" Magda cried as she ran to the woman, with Leah rushing behind her. The girls put their arms around Esther's waist.

Joshua saw Esther's surprise. She could have been upset since her arms were full, but she laughed with pleasure instead as she put the platters down inside the buggy so she could return his girls' hugs.

"I didn't see you arrive," Esther said with a grin. She glanced toward his parents and the twins. "*Gut* morning!"

When he locked gazes with her, Joshua saw her smile. Something shifted inside him, a warmth that was pleasurable and totally unexpected. He felt his lips curve upward in response—he was drawn to her, an attraction that startled him.

Esther returned her attention to the girls. "You want to carry in food for Fannie?"

"*Ja!*" Magda and Leah exclaimed together.

She reached back inside her buggy and handed a plastic container to Magda and another one to Leah. Joshua reached the three of them as Esther went to retrieve the two serving dishes she'd held before his girls had startled her.

"You're here early," he said softly. He wondered if he should offer to carry something for her. Although he still used his cane, he knew his legs had strengthened after two and a half weeks of physical therapy.

Esther nodded. "I picked up food for Fannie from the restaurant."

"That was kind of you," he said, watching as his girls entered the house with a grinning Fannie holding the door open for them. His father and Alta followed with the twins and went in behind them.

"It's about time you got here, bruder!" Fannie called out after the others had gone inside. "There's still time for me to show you the *haus*."

"I'll be there in a moment." Joshua focused his attention on Esther. "If there is more you need to bring inside, I can carry it for you. I'm stronger than I look," he added, anticipating her objection.

Esther studied him thoughtfully. "*Okey*."

He raised his eyebrows. "*Okey?*"

"That's what I said." She jerked her head toward her buggy. "The box on the back seat. Paper plates and plastic utensils."

"You don't want me to take anything else?" He reached inside for a good-sized box, but it was light because of its contents.

She frowned. "Don't you need one hand free?" she asked, pointedly eyeing his cane.

He hooked his cane over his arm. "I have a free one now."

"Joshua…"

"I'm fine, Esther. The only reason I'm still using it is because I haven't asked my therapist if I can get rid of it yet." Joshua continued to hold her gaze.

"I don't want you to get hurt," she whispered.

"I won't." He waited until she handed him a foil-wrapped dish to carry. Joshua started toward the house with his hands full as the door opened. His sister watched his approach.

"I'm glad you came," Fannie said as she held it open. She frowned. "Your cane doesn't help when it's over your arm."

"I don't need it." He carried the box and dish inside. "Where do you want these?"

Esther chuckled as she came in after him. "I basically told him the same thing," she quipped as she left the kitchen with his daughters following her.

"Put it on the table." His sister gestured toward a specific spot.

Joshua set the box and dish down then went to the window when he heard buggy wheels outside. "You can show me the *haus* later. Church members are beginning to arrive." He watched as the buggy parked and then grinned as his twin brothers, Danny and DJ, climbed out and headed toward the house. Danny held a covered basket and DJ a plastic container.

His brothers entered the house. Danny saw him first. "If it isn't the old man!" he said in greeting.

"Haven't seen you since the day you moved into your *haus*," DJ said, setting the plastic container on the table. Danny placed the basket next to it.

Joshua shrugged. "You weren't at the last church service."

"You're lucky we decided to come here today," Danny said. "You know we don't live in this church district. But we like to attend whenever we get a hankering to see family. And we haven't seen you on Visiting Day either."

"Haven't been yet, but I will be there next time." Joshua felt confident now that his leg was doing well and he felt steadier.

"Don't know if we'll make it then," DJ teased.

"Your loss," Joshua retorted with a laugh. Joking with his younger brothers raised his spirits.

Esther reentered the kitchen with his girls. "Look what the cat dragged in," she said with a grin.

Danny laughed. "Esther! You're a sight for sore eyes."

"It's been too long since we've seen you," DJ added with delight in his expression.

Joshua was shocked to feel a stab of envy that she was clearly at ease with his brothers. He wished she'd feel that comfortable with him, but his grumpiness might have made things awkward between them.

Since she'd come into his life, Esther had been there for his children and him. He realized that he felt protective of his relationship with her. His *dat* hinted that Esther might be the one who would make him a good wife. And he realized then that he'd begun to feel the same way. He couldn't replace Anna in his heart, but he couldn't deny that Esther already fit into his household. But he was concerned, since she was a young woman who probably wanted children of her own. All he could offer her was a marriage of convenience with him as her husband and his children to mother.

Joshua frowned. Why hadn't she married? He never thought to ask Fannie whether Esther had a man in her life. He suffered a tightening in his chest at the possibility. Yet if Esther had a betrothed or someone special, his father wouldn't have encouraged him to consider her as his wife.

It was wrong for him to offer so little when Esther would need to give up so much. But she had a special way with his children, and her care had made their new house feel like a home these past few weeks. He would regret it if he didn't at least ask her.

Soon family and friends filled Fannie's house, and everyone proceeded into an area that was large enough for the congregation. The space was two rooms with the separating wall that slid open, which made it a huge one perfect for church.

Alta and Esther brought his children to sit with them in the women's section. Joshua took a seat with the men, and as service started, he couldn't keep his gaze away from Esther and how she interacted with his daughters and sons.

Multiple hymns and sermons followed, including one given by his father, and then church was done. It was time for the midday meal. The women carried food to two long tables at one end of the room, while the men hurried to shift benches around others for dining.

Joshua pitched in to help, despite the vocal concern of his father and his brother-in-law, David. At Fannie's urging, the men sat down, and the women served their meals. He preferred when the weather was nice. In the warmth of spring and summer, the men and their families would eat together outside.

It didn't feel right to have his children wait until he and the other men were done. Joshua waved Esther over. "I wish the children could sit with us." He meant Esther and him—not the other men.

Esther smiled. "That can be arranged. They're in Rose's room playing quietly with the twins. I'll get them for you." She turned to leave.

"Esther," he said impulsively, stopping her.

She stiffened then faced him. "*Ja?*"

"I'd like to talk with you later," he said.

She appeared worried. "Is anything wrong?"

"*Nay.*" He softened inside and smiled. "I'd simply like a word."

The tension eased from her expression. "*Oll recht.*"

After Esther left the room, Joshua noticed his brother-in-law standing near Fannie, holding their daughter, Rose. He smiled. David was a fine man who clearly wanted what he did—to eat with his wife and child. Except he wanted to eat with his little ones and Esther.

Several of the men rose simultaneously from the table. "We're going to head out to the barn," his *dat* said.

"*Okey,* Vadder," Fannie said after a quick look at her husband, who nodded his permission with a smile.

His *dat* went outside with the others to the outbuilding to have male conversations, no doubt about the weather, what they planned to do for the holidays and the crops they hoped to plant in the spring. Esther returned with his children. Joshua took the twins and sat one on each side of him. Magda grinned when he gestured toward the seats across from him.

"Please join us," Joshua urged Esther with a smile. He saw her eyes widen slightly before she shot a glance toward a table of women across the room, where her mother and sister were seated. Then she sat down, facing him, with Magda on her one side and Leah on the other.

Fannie put food on a plate for her daughter and filled David's. Joshua noted the love between them as their gazes locked, and David thanked her with a soft smile. He felt a rush of sorrow as he recalled how it had been with Anna. He attempted to put aside his grief, but it was difficult. In death, Anna was lost to him. What mattered now were his children, who needed a mother.

Platters of cold beef and dishes of sweet-and-sour green beans were passed around, and everyone took a portion of each. Rose sat next to JJ, and the cousins grinned at each other, seeming to talk in a language all their own. Esther helped his little girls get whatever they wanted. More cold meat and side dishes were distributed, and then all of them chatted while they ate.

Watching Esther, Joshua liked the way she mothered his little ones. She'd be at his house tomorrow to babysit while he went for his appointment. And she'd be back two other times this week.

Joshua knew by the way she treated them that she would

be a wonderful *mam*. But could he do it? Convince her to marry him when he had nothing to offer her except his children and a home?

When they had finished eating the main meal, Esther rose and brought over brownies, cookies and pie for them to choose from and enjoy.

Joshua watched with a smile as she passed out paper plates and helped the children with their dessert selection. Then Esther and Fannie left the room with the leftover food, leaving fathers and little ones to enjoy the baked treats together.

In the kitchen, Esther covered the platter of roast beef and found a place for it in Fannie's refrigerator.

"You seem to be getting along with my *bruder* and his *kinner*." Using aluminum foil, Fannie covered a bowl of dried corn casserole that had been reheated on the woodstove before the midday meal. "I take it the cleaning job is going well?"

"*Ja*, Fannie, it's going fine," Esther admitted, "but it doesn't seem right to abandon you at the restaurant."

Her friend spun around from the counter and placed her hands on her hips. "I told you I'd prefer it if you help Joshua." She tucked a strand of blond hair under her *kapp*. "How many times do I have to tell you?" Her tone was firm but not angry.

"If you're certain—"

Fannie shook her head as if frustrated. "When will you learn I mean what I say?" she asked kindly.

A sound made Esther glance toward the doorway that led to the church room. Half expecting to see Joshua, she saw instead that it was her mother and sister. Her *mam* held two uneaten pies while Linda brought in the last of the brownies.

Fannie smiled at them. "*Danki*. If you'd put them on the table until we can wrap them, I'd appreciate it."

Esther felt an odd flutter in her belly when her *mam* and *schweschter* brushed past her as they took the desserts to the table. Did they wonder why she'd chosen to sit with Joshua and his children? *Please don't ask.* She watched as they set down the dishes and faced her.

"Joshua's adorable little girls are asking for you," her *mam* said. "You may want to go in to see them."

Hoping that her *mam* didn't notice the heat in her cheeks, Esther nodded. "I'll go check on them now."

"Esther," her mother said.

She paused and looked back at her. "*Ja,* Mam?"

"We're going home," her *mam* said. "We'll see you later."

Esther nodded without a word, then continued toward the other room where Joshua still sat with his children, his brother-in-law and David's daughter.

"Esther," Magda cried when she caught sight of Esther entering the room.

Noting the little girl's upset expression, she frowned. "What's wrong?" She met Joshua's gaze. "What's happened?" Then she saw one of the twins cradled in his father's arms.

"Jacob has a tummy ache," he said with concern as he studied his little boy. "Too many desserts, I think."

"Joshua, we'll take you home," Alta offered as she approached with a breadbasket and plate of butter from another table. "I'll get your *vadder.*"

"No need, Alta." Esther smiled. "I came alone this morning. I'll be happy to take them."

Alta looked hesitant, as if debating whether Esther's offer was a good idea.

"*Ja,* Mam. We can go back with Esther," Joshua said, and Esther saw Alta's surprised but pleased expression. As if this was the first time that Joshua had called her *mother.*

"*Okey,*" Alta said. "I'll stay then and visit with Fannie until your *vadder* is ready to leave."

Magda got up from the table and took Leah's hand. Esther reached for JJ while Joshua stood, holding Jacob close.

Esther led the way outside to where she'd parked her buggy after unloading the food.

Joshua and his young ones followed her to her buggy. After helping the girls and JJ into the back, she started to get onto the driver's seat then changed her mind. "I thought maybe you'd like to drive." She reached for the child in his father's arms. "I'll hold and cuddle Jacob."

Joshua appeared surprised, then his brown eyes seemed to soften as he nodded. After she got in first with Jacob, he climbed in after her. A quick glance at the girls made Esther smile. Magda had stepped up as big sister with her arm around JJ's shoulders. Leah was on her brother's other side, holding his little hand.

Joshua steered the horse-drawn buggy onto the road and made a right turn toward home. Seated next to him, Esther felt an odd sense of contentment as she kept Jacob protectively on her lap during the ride.

This is what it would be like to have a husband and children of my own. When sadness threatened to take away this moment of happiness, Esther closed her eyes and fought it.

Think about now, and those brief moments of joy spending time with Joshua and his little ones. I must take my happiness wherever I can find it, for the future of a fam-

ily isn't available for me. How can it be when I can't give a husband children?

Esther ran her fingers through little Jacob's hair. "It will be *oll recht*," she whispered with tears suddenly filling her eyes.

She knew the moment Joshua looked her way, as if sensing her mood.

"Are you *okey*?" he asked, his deep voice rippling down her spine.

"*Ja*." Esther managed a genuine smile for him. "I'm fine. I'm just worried about Jacob."

She dipped her head, aware that Joshua studied her a little longer before turning his attention back to the road. The man had said he needed to talk with her. Probably just to remind her what time to be at the house to babysit.

Jacob had fallen asleep. Inhaling his sweet scent, she cuddled the little boy close and tried to shut off her mind.

Chapter Eight

"Esther," a deep male voice said. "We're here."

Esther blinked, painfully aware that she'd closed her eyes briefly during the ride home from church. She hugged the child in her arms and opened her eyes to see Joshua beside her in the driver's seat of the buggy, gazing at her with amusement. She felt her cheeks heat. "I wasn't sleeping. My eyes were closed for only a few seconds."

Joshua smiled. "I could tell you were awake."

"Do you still want me to babysit tomorrow?" Esther shifted the little boy in her arms to make sure he was comfortable.

"*Ja*, it would be a big help if you could. Can you come around nine?" As Joshua checked the back seat, Esther knew he'd see his daughters with their eyes closed, a sleeping JJ between them.

"I'll be there at nine." She felt a rush of pleasure at the prospect of spending time with his little ones. "I'll help you get them into the *haus* and settled."

Joshua climbed out of his vehicle then reached in to grab his cane. Esther slipped out behind him, holding Jacob carefully in her arms.

She listened to his smooth, loving tone as he woke up the children in the back seat, starting with Magda. His eldest child got out of the buggy and assisted her baby brother. Leah climbed out after the other two. Joshua picked up JJ, and they all started toward the house with Joshua in the lead. Esther trailed behind them with Jacob. She gazed at the little boy in her arms and smiled when she saw that he hadn't stirred.

Magda ran ahead to open the door, and Esther stood back as Joshua entered the house carrying JJ with Leah following. Joshua's oldest child continued to hold the door until Esther went inside with Jacob.

When she didn't see Joshua immediately, Esther realized that he must have gone into the twins' room. She headed there with Jacob in time to see the twins' father pull a quilt over JJ, who lay curled on his side as he slept. She put Jacob in his bed. After she pulled the boy's quilt up to his waist, she stood a moment to watch him sleeping peacefully. A sudden tingle at the nape of her neck alerted her that Joshua was close before he joined her beside Jacob's crib.

"Amazing to see them quietly sleeping," he said gruffly after several seconds of silence. "They can be a handful when they're awake and running about the *haus*."

Esther turned to study him. "Magda does a *wunderbor* job of keeping them occupied in the mornings."

"*Ja,* she is a nurturer." Joshua seemed thoughtful. "Like her *mudder* was."

Recognizing pain in his voice, Esther had no idea how to respond. She waited a heartbeat, wondering if he would say more. When he didn't, she said, "I should get back to Fannie's to see if she needs me."

"She won't." He faced her briefly, his expression unreadable, before he returned his attention to Jacob. "She had plenty of help when we left."

"I'll head home then." But Esther found herself in no

hurry to leave. She suddenly recalled that he had wanted to have a conversation with her. "You said you wanted to talk with me. Was it to remind me what time to be here in the morning?"

He met her gaze. Joshua opened his mouth as if to say something more but then he nodded instead. Confused by his behavior, she managed a smile. "I'll be here early enough to give you plenty of time to get to your appointment in case there is traffic."

He returned her smile. "That would be *gut. Danki.*"

"You're *willkomm.* I'll see you then." Esther stopped briefly on her way out to add two logs to the banked fire in the woodstove. "I'm heading home," she told Magda when she saw her.

"Will you be here tomorrow?" The child followed Esther into the kitchen.

Esther paused to reassure her with a smile. "*Ja.* I'll be here with you whenever your *dat* has PT appointments this week." She placed her hand lovingly on Magda's head. "I'll see you in the morning."

And then she left, her thoughts filled with the man of the house and his adorable children, all of whom had come to mean a lot to her. *Careful*, she warned herself. *He's grieving for his late wife. The last thing I want him to find out is that I'm falling for him.* It was a mistake for her to think of him as anything but a friend, but she still couldn't seem to keep herself from feeling more for him each moment she spent in his company. And even if things had been different, the fact remained that she was infertile because of her medical issues. If Joshua married again, he would most likely want another child, if not more, since Amish men liked large families. Sons to help with their father's chores and daughters to work in the house once they were old enough.

* * *

The next morning, Joshua was up well before dawn after a sleepless night. He couldn't stop thinking about doing the best thing for his children.

Your kinner can't wait until you are ready to marry. His father's words echoed in his mind, making him realize the truth. Magda, Leah, JJ and Jacob needed a mother. And Esther would be a wonderful *mam*. He knew she loved his children. He could see it in her interactions with them. And he liked Esther. A lot.

Today, he would ask her to become his wife. It would be a marriage of convenience only because it didn't feel right for him to fall in love again after losing Anna.

Asking Esther to marry him made him ridiculously nervous. He'd never worried this much during his early courtship with Anna. But then he'd never proposed a marriage of convenience before either.

As he sipped his coffee, he heard noise near his back door. He rose and went to the window, and was surprised by what he saw. Esther placed a basket on his back stoop and started back toward her buggy. The time had come. He had to stop her from leaving.

Joshua threw open the door. "Esther!" His voice was low but loud enough for her to have heard him.

She spun around and looked startled to see him. "I didn't mean to disturb you so early."

"I've been up for a while. Come inside." He opened the door wider in invitation. "I have coffee ready."

Esther seemed to hesitate before she moved in his direction. She retrieved the cloth-covered basket from his stoop and entered the house while he held the door open for her. After setting it on the kitchen table, she took off her coat and hung it up. "I was up early and made muffins for you and your *kinner*. I know I'll be back later, but I wanted to make sure you had something for breakfast before I got here."

"Coffee *oll recht*?" He found a sudden sense of calm as he pulled down a mug for her. "Or would you rather have tea?"

She came up beside him. "Coffee is fine." She reached for the mug. "I can do it. Would you like a refill?"

Joshua eyed her with amusement. "I can handle pouring you coffee," he said quietly. "Did you think I couldn't?"

"*Ach, nay,* that's not what I thought!" Esther exclaimed, blushing delightfully when she met his gaze.

He found himself chuckling. "You do a lot for us, Esther. I want to do something nice for you."

Her face turned a brighter shade of red. "*Ach*… I—"

"It's fine." He gazed at her with fondness. Joshua poured two cups of coffee and turned to see Esther pull the cloth off the basket. Nestled inside were at least a dozen muffins.

They sipped from their drinks quietly. "Two flavors of muffins?" he asked.

"*Ja,* nine of each. Sweet muffins and chocolate." She grinned. "The chocolate ones are for you." She placed one on a napkin and handed it to him. "I remember how much you like chocolate cake so I thought you might enjoy these."

Joshua took a bite, and the delicious burst of chocolate flavor teased and satisfied his taste buds. "*Danki.* This is delicious."

"You're *willkomm*." She chose a sweet muffin for herself. He watched as Esther bit into the muffin and closed her eyes, clearly enjoying the breakfast treat.

"What if I hadn't found these before you got here?" he asked, curious about why she'd delivered them in the early hours of a dark November morning.

Esther shrugged. "I would have called you a little later and told you where to find them."

He chuckled. "Wise woman," he said sincerely, and she beamed at him. He took a sip from his mug and set it down. It was now or never, he thought. "I'm glad you're here before the children got up. There is something I want to discuss with you. It's a bit unconventional, but…"

She gazed at him with nothing but mild curiosity. "*Okey.*"

Joshua ran his fingers through his hair as he strived for the right thing to say. "As you must have learned by now, I lost my wife over seven months ago."

"*Ja.*" Her green eyes filled with sympathy as Esther studied him. "I'm sure that has been hard for you and your *kinner.*"

"It has been." He paused, wondering how best to phrase his request. "Magda and Leah are *gut* girls and have stepped up to help with their baby *bruders.*" When Esther nodded, Joshua was encouraged to go on. "My little ones need a *mam*, and well… I'd like her to be you. But I need to be honest and forthcoming, Esther," he added when he saw her surprised expression. "What I'm offering is a marriage of convenience. If you agree to be my wife, you'll have a home with us and children to care for. I know it's not fair to ask this of you since I can't promise more." He swallowed against a lump in his throat. "If you agree, we'll be friends raising the children together. Anything I have will be yours…except my heart. I'll understand if you say *nay.*"

And then he waited for what felt like forever for her to respond, as it had become vitally important to him that she say yes.

Esther was stunned by his proposal. He wanted to marry her. Not a real marriage. But he'd be her husband, even if in name only, and she'd be a mother to his children. Her thoughts raced as she struggled over how to respond. She would be risking her heart if she accepted his offer, but she would gain so much more. Still, there were other things she needed to consider before she gave him her answer. "May I think about it for a couple of days?"

He blinked and appeared astonished that she hadn't immediately rejected his offer. "*Ja,* of course."

Heart beating wildly, Esther realized that she was going to seriously consider it. She had always wanted a family of her own. Of course, she'd imagined herself married to a man who loved her, but she had given up that ideal long ago. Was she willing to tie herself to a man who would never love her even though she got to be a mother if they wed? She wasn't sure how she felt about it. "I'll give you my answer by Wednesday."

"*Okey.*" His brown eyes regarded her intently, making her slightly uneasy.

She pushed back her chair and stood. "I should get home. My family doesn't know I left."

Joshua opened his mouth, and Esther thought he might scold her, but he didn't.

"Everyone was still sleeping." Esther put on her coat. "I'll be back before nine."

She climbed into her buggy then glanced toward the house. Joshua stood at the window, watching her. Heart pounding, she waved to him and then left, her mind grappling with whether she should accept his offer.

Chapter Nine

"Can we help fold clothes?" Leah asked as she preceded Magda into the room. The twins had been put down for their nap.

"*Ja,* of course." Esther shifted the laundry basket on the kitchen table to within the girls' reach. She showed them how to sort socks and put them together, and then watched with fondness as they folded more, doing a good job.

Magda took out their dresses. "We'll hang these in our room."

"That would be *wunderbor.*" She shook out one of Joshua's shirts—a green one—and laid it carefully next to the basket. "Would you please check to see if your *bruders* are sleeping?"

"*Okey,*" Magda said, "and if they are, we'll stay in our room to work on puzzles together."

Esther finished with the laundry and went to put away Joshua's clothes. While she was there, she looked in the boys' bedroom. The twins were asleep, and she quietly closed their door so they wouldn't be disturbed. She peeked in on the girls and studied them a moment while they sat on the floor with a stack of wooden puzzles before them. Their heads were bent as they worked on one together.

The house was warm and cozy. Esther made herself a

cup of tea and sat down at the table to enjoy it in silence. Immediately, the image of the children's father filled her thoughts. Joshua had been pleasant when she'd arrived to babysit this morning. Nothing in his manner suggested that he'd even recalled the proposal he'd made her earlier. For her, however, she'd thought of little else since then but becoming his wife. She'd understood what he was offering. He would marry her, provide for her and give her his children to mother and cuddle, but she would never have his heart. Was she crazy for considering it?

Nay, she thought, because she knew she'd never marry otherwise. If another man had asked her to wed, she'd have to tell him the truth—that she could never give him children because she was barren. And to the men in the Amish community, it was imperative that a woman give her husband sons and daughters, that they create a family together.

A marriage to Joshua, even one in name only, would allow her to have that family she longed for. And she trusted him. He was a wonderful father and she knew he'd be a good husband.

If I agree to the arrangement, the only thing I must insist on is that only the two of us will ever know that our marriage isn't a true one.

No one knew about the medical condition that prevented her from conceiving a child. Which was why she never attended singings or actively engaged with the young men within her church community, because of the embarrassment, the heartbreak, it would bring if anyone found out that she couldn't have children. When she hadn't shown interest in any boys, her parents had worried. Her sister, Linda, knew that Esther had a problem with cramps, but she didn't know the whole truth of why. Esther's pain was sometimes strong enough that she had to resort to using the *Englisher* method of pain relief—ibuprofen or acet-aminophen, depending on its severity. Linda thought that Esther suffered because of her monthly cycle. And in the past, while her sister had encouraged her to attend youth singings, Linda no longer insisted she come.

Esther had refused to agree to be operated on for her en-dometriosis since the medicine was managing her pain well so far. She didn't want to risk an operation when she could deal with it on her own, even if she suffered sometimes.

A short while later, the door opened, signaling Joshua's return home from his appointment. He entered the house unaided and leaned his cane against the wall near the door.

Esther met his gaze with a smile. "*Gut* news?" she asked when he walked to the table without issue.

His lips curved. "*Ja.* I don't need the cane anymore. And after Wednesday's session, I'll be done with physi-cal therapy."

"Congratulations." Esther watched him hang up his coat. "There is hot water on the stove. Would like some tea?"

"Please." He fetched a cup from a cabinet, while Es-ther pulled out tea bags from a tin on the counter. Turning with mug in hand, he smiled at her. "Are you in a hurry to leave or can you stay and join me?" Joshua took the seat next to hers.

"I can stay. I don't have to go into work today." She poured hot water into their mugs. Since his proposal this morning, Esther couldn't stop thinking about what it would be like to be Joshua's wife. Another woman would prob-ably have told him *nay* immediately, but she wasn't one to reject him out of hand. She knew he'd provide for her and the children, and being a part of their lives seemed like an answer to her prayers. Although she'd asked him for time to think about it, she was ready to give him her answer.

She knew she'd be risking her heart, but she was willing to take a chance. Now she just had to bring up the subject and hope that he hadn't changed his mind.

"Are the children napping?" he asked.

"The twins are. Your girls are in their room playing quietly." As she thought of them, she smiled and added sugar to her tea after he had spooned some into his. "They seemed tired, too, so it's likely that they've decided to lie down."

Joshua took a sip from his tea and seemed satisfied with its taste. "Did everyone behave?"

"*Ja.* They were *wunderbor.*" She took a drink as she garnered the courage to start a discussion about his proposal. "Joshua, about this morning…"

His expression became unreadable, almost as if expecting her to reject the idea of marrying him. "*Ja,* what about it?"

"I've thought about your offer of marriage," she began, immediately noting the tension in his face and body. "I've decided to accept it."

He frowned. "Wait! *What?* Did you just agree to marry me?"

Esther nodded, amused at his shocked expression. "*Ja,* I will if you want this. And I'm fine with the fact that ours will be a marriage of convenience only, but—" She felt captured by the intensity in his brown eyes.

"But?" He leaned closer to her, and she detected the pleasing scent that belonged only to him. A scent she enjoyed and loved.

"There is one thing I must insist on." Her hands shook and she placed them in her lap to steady them. "No one but us can ever know that ours is not a real marriage."

She heard his sigh of relief. "Esther, I have no intention of telling anyone what's between us," he said softly. "You'll be my wife and that's the only thing that matters. Our relationship is no one's business but ours."

Esther closed her eyes briefly. When she reopened them, she saw approval in his warm brown gaze. To her relief, he looked relaxed and pleased. "*Danki*."

"There is no need to thank me, Esther." His voice was quiet, almost affectionate. "I'm honored by your faith in me, in us, in the future, and I'm grateful that you agreed to be my wife and my children's *mudder*."

Esther felt a fluttering in her stomach. "When do you want us to wed?"

"As soon as possible. I'd like us to be a family before Christmas." He studied her carefully, in a way that made her self-conscious. "How old are you?"

She chuckled. "Twenty-three. I'll be twenty-four on Christmas Day."

He grinned. "Another reason to celebrate the holiday." Joshua paused for a quick sip of tea. "Aren't you going to ask my age?"

"I know how old you are. Fannie mentioned it when she told me you were moving back home." Esther smirked. "You're twenty-eight."

"I am," he said.

Esther pushed back her chair and stood. "There are still muffins left. The children had one each for a snack. Magda made sure to save the chocolate for you."

Joshua laughed. "She knows me too well."

After arranging several of the breakfast treats on a plate, she carried them, along with the butter dish, paper plates and napkins, to the table.

Joshua grabbed his favorite flavor and took a bite. He put down the muffin and eyed her as if seeing her for the first time. "Why aren't you betrothed? You are a lovely young woman. I don't understand why some man hasn't already staked a claim on you."

She blushed. "No one here has taken my fancy." Her face burned with heat.

He looked thoughtful. "Their loss, my gain. I'll talk with my *vadder* since he is a church elder." Joshua hesitated. "I imagine you want a big wedding with our congregation. We may have to wait until the banns are read at church service."

Esther shook her head. "I don't need a big wedding. A quiet ceremony with our church elders and family will be enough…" She bit her lip. "If they'll allow it."

"I'm certain they will." Pleased that Esther had made up her mind quickly, Joshua grew thoughtful. He was sure that they'd be able to marry when and however they wanted. He was a widower—and therefore exempt from the rules of marriage for young couples—and his father was a preacher. He knew his *dat* would back him in whatever decision he and Esther made together. "Dat and Alta will be home on Friday, and I'll talk with my *vadder* then."

"*Oll recht.*" Esther finished her last swallow of tea and stood. She took her mug to the sink and washed it before placing it on a rack to dry. "I need to get home. There are things I need to do for my *mam*. Tomorrow I'll be back at Fannie's Luncheonette."

He frowned. "You know you won't need to work after we're married."

Esther appeared surprised by his statement. But it made sense, he thought.

"The children," he pointed out, arching his eyebrows.

She laughed. "Of course, I'll be here for your *kinner*." She paused. "And you."

"*Gut.*" Joshua beamed at her. "It's been years since I lived in New Berne. Can you tell me who the current bishop is?"

"David Bontrager," she told him. "He was selected for the position recently, after John Hostetler, our last one, passed on."

He nodded. Joshua thought about approaching the bishop first to ensure that they had permission for the simpler marriage ceremony that Esther wanted—and that he felt was best. Although he wanted to tell his children that Esther would be their *mam* soon, he couldn't yet…not until their union was approved.

"We won't tell the children until everything is arranged. Is that *oll recht*?" He examined her features and found only acceptance.

"*Ja,* that's *gut.*" She looked at him. "Do you want another muffin?"

He shook his head. "This is a perfect snack. *Danki.*"

Esther smiled and put away the muffins before she returned to the table to reach for his empty mug. "Another?"

"I'd appreciate it." He was extremely happy that she'd agreed to be his wife. He would do everything he could to make sure she was content, despite that his heart would always be Anna's.

She handed him his refill. "I should go. I'll see you on Wednesday."

"*Ja, danki.*" He smiled, pleased with the progress he'd made in physical therapy in such a short time. "My last appointment."

Joshua stood and reached to the wall hook for her coat before she got a chance to grab it. He held it open for her, waiting patiently while she inserted her arms into the woolen sleeves. She pulled the ends of the garment closed, and he nodded with approval. "I'm glad your coat is warm. It's cold outside."

She blushed. "It is." Esther left and Joshua found himself watching her through the window. She didn't turn to acknowledge him or wave as she climbed into her buggy. Only once did she look toward the house before she drove away, but he figured she hadn't seen him because he'd stepped back behind the curtains.

Joshua experienced a rush of relief that his prayers had been answered and Esther would soon be a mother to his children. *And my wife.*

Chapter Ten

❧

"I asked Esther to marry me, and she said *ja*," Joshua said when his father arrived to pick up his children for a visit late Friday morning. His *dat* and Alta had returned home yesterday, a day earlier than expected.

"That's *wunderbor*, soohn!" His *dat* was clearly delighted.

Joshua nodded in agreement. "She's a lovely young woman who will make me a fine wife. And she loves my *kinner* as much as I do."

"Yet you seem worried." Jonas Miller had always been tuned in to the concerns of his children. "What's wrong?"

He nodded hesitantly. "I was going to talk with the bishop, but then I thought it would be best if I run this by you first." Joshua paused as he tried to figure out the right way to word his betrothed's request. "Esther and I would like to have a small wedding with only family and our church elders. We wish to be married before Christmas so that we can spend the holidays as a family. We're concerned about the banns. If we wait the usual amount of time for them, the wedding can't take place until well after the Christmas holidays." He ran a hand nervously through his dark hair. "Is it possible for us to skip them? Everyone knows I'm a widower, and Esther has never been married. There is nothing to keep us apart but time and convention."

His father looked thoughtful. "Let me talk with David, our bishop, to see if he'll allow us to have the banns changed to one week at our next church service instead of three that is the usual for a young couple marrying. If they allow it, then you can marry whenever you'd like after that. A church elder must still visit Esther's parents and ask permission for you to marry their daughter. If it's *oll recht* with you, I'll talk with them. They have known me for years. We are *gut* friends." He smiled. "I'm sure they'll be pleased for you and Esther to wed."

"I hope so. *Danki,* Dat." He heard his children in the living room. "Magda, Leah, your *grossdaddi* is here," he called. "Will you get your *bruders*?"

Leah ran into the room first. "Grossdaddi! We haven't seen you in a long time. Dat said you've been away."

Jonas grinned. "We have. But we're home now and thought you might like to have lunch with us."

"*Okey!* I need to help Magda with JJ and Jacob!" Leah started to run from the room.

"No running," Joshua said, and then he chuckled, pleased, when his youngest daughter slowed to a walk.

"You have *gut kinner*, Joshua." His father took Magda's coat from him while Joshua held Leah's garment. "You're a fine *vadder,* never doubt that."

"I love them." Joshua glanced toward the doorway where Magda appeared with Jacob.

"It's easy to see how much." Jonas picked up Jacob and handed Magda her coat. When Magda ran to help her sister with JJ, his father smiled. "Esther will make your family complete. She's a fine woman and I've watched her with your children. She will be a *gut* mother."

Joshua nodded, but at the same time, it was hard to shake his guilt at the thought of another woman taking over the care of Anna's babies.

"All ready to go?" Jonas asked after his grandchildren had put on their coats.

"*Ja,* we're ready!" Leah exclaimed.

Joshua's father caught and held his gaze. "I'll let you know what the elders decide."

He nodded, but until the marriage and conditions were approved, Joshua would continue to worry.

"Dat?" Leah looked up at him with bright blue eyes. "Is Esther coming today?"

"*Nay,* not today, dochter. I've finished with my doctor's appointments." He gave her an affectionate smile. "But we'll see her again soon."

"You'll see her on Thanksgiving," Jonas assured her. "She and her family will be at our *haus* for dinner."

"When is Thanksgiving?" Magda held firm to JJ's hand as the little boy struggled to get free.

"Next Thursday." Joshua adjusted JJ's navy blue woolen cap so his little ears were protected from the cold. "It's less than a week away."

"Try not to fret, soohn," his *dat* said over his shoulder as he and his grandchildren headed for the door. "All will be well."

Esther was upstairs in her mother's craft room, using her sewing machine. This Saturday afternoon, she was finishing up Christmas presents for Joshua's daughters—new black bonnets to wear over their *kapps* to keep them warm throughout the winter months ahead.

"Esther!" her *mam* called. "Would you come down here for a moment?"

"Be right there, Mam!" She put the bonnets into a cloth bag and cleaned up her mother's valued workspace. After tossing the bag into her room, she went downstairs. "What do you need?" she asked as she entered the kitchen. Esther froze. Her mother and father were seated with Preacher Jonas, Joshua's *dat*.

"Have a seat, dochter." Her father gestured to an empty chair, and she slid onto it, feeling suddenly nervous as she studied each adult in the room.

"Is something wrong?" she asked, placing her trembling hands in her lap.

"That depends on you," Mam said.

She swallowed against a tight throat. "I don't understand."

"Preacher Jonas has come to us with a request," Dat said, watching her closely. "He tells us that his *soohn* Joshua wants to marry you."

Esther didn't say a word. Was he denying his permission? His blessing? Would her *vadder* refuse their marriage because she hadn't known him long enough?

"Esther," her father said. "Do you want to wed Joshua Miller?"

Transferring her gaze briefly to Jonas, she gave a nod. "I do. I want to marry him."

The tension seemed to leave the room. "I see," her *dat* said. He exchanged looks with her mother. "In that case, Preacher, I'm happy to give Joshua our permission, and our blessing, to wed our *dochter*."

Jonas eyed her with softness in his brown eyes that were so like his son's. "I'll let him know."

"About the wedding," her *mam* said. "Jonas tells us that you and Joshua want a simple ceremony with only family and our church elders." She paused. "Is that true?"

"*Ja.* We thought it best," Esther told her parents calmly.

"We want to be man and wife before Christmas. I'm looking forward to spending the holidays with my new husband and our *kinner*."

"I see." Dat nodded. "That's fine then. What day were you thinking?"

"I'd like to talk with Joshua so we can decide together." Esther stood. "If it's *okey*, I'll give him a call and make plans to discuss it with him. I don't think you have to worry about having enough time to prepare since we are keeping it simple."

"I'm sure you're *recht*," her father said with a small smile.

She started to leave the room to call Joshua but then stopped to face Jonas and her parents. "*Danki*," she said sincerely.

"There is no need to thank us, dochter." Her *dat* gazed at her with affection. "We only want you to be happy, and if Joshua is the man who can do that, we are more than pleased to *willkomm* him into our family and our hearts."

With a smile, she nodded and left the room. It took only a minute before she got Joshua on the phone. "My *eldre* have given us their blessing," she said as soon as he answered.

"That's *wunderbor*, Esther."

"They need a date," she said. "I'd like to come over now to discuss it if that's *oll recht*."

"Is my *vadder* still there?" he asked.

She frowned. "*Ja*. Why?"

"Have him drive you." Joshua's voice was a low rumble over the phone line. "I'll take you home after we talk."

"*Oll recht*." After she hung up, Esther stared at the wall as she recalled her conversation with Joshua. Her husband-to-be had sounded pleased at first, but then something about his tone changed, and she was worried. She returned to the kitchen and told Jonas of his son's request. The preacher was only too happy to take her.

Soon, she was in Jonas's buggy heading toward the one-level house that belonged to Joshua Miller, her betrothed. At least, he would be if he hadn't changed his mind.

Esther inwardly scolded herself as Jonas pulled onto the road where Joshua lived. The man had proposed to her. He wouldn't have asked her to marry him if he didn't want to go through with the wedding. She sat up straighter, calmer at the realization, as her future father-in-law turned onto his son's driveway.

"I'm pleased that you'll be my boy's wife, Esther."

She smiled. "I am, too."

As she approached the house, Joshua opened the door. He waved to his father before he stepped back. "Come in, Esther."

She moved farther into the kitchen as he shut the door. When she faced him, his expression made her sigh with relief. There was warmth in his brown eyes as he met her gaze. He still wanted their marriage. *Thank Gott*, she thought.

"We have a lot to discuss," he said softly.

Esther nodded. "We do." She stepped inside and closed the door behind her.

The day was clear and sunny without a breeze but with a nip in the air that reminded Joshua that it would soon be winter. As he drove his buggy to his parents' house for Thanksgiving, he wondered how the rest of their family members would react to his and Esther's decision to keep their wedding simple. He'd seen his betrothed only once since they'd discussed the date. When he'd driven her home last Saturday, he'd felt something he hadn't expected—

warmth and strong developing feelings for the woman who was to become his wife. Intrigued by his fiancée, he'd been unable to get her out of his mind—not even for a second. Now it was five days later, and he was surprised by how much he looked forwarded to seeing her again.

"Dat, are we having turkey today?" Magda asked from the back seat. Ever the young nurturer, she preferred to sit with her siblings and keep her baby brothers calm, a feat which was getting harder to do. His sons were getting more active and more difficult to distract by the day.

"*Ja,* turkey and all the trimmings." He kept his eyes focused on his driving so he wouldn't miss the turnoff that would take him to his parents' house.

"You mean like stuffing and mashed potatoes and other yummy dishes?" Leah leaned forward over the back of the front seat.

"That's exactly what I mean." Joshua viewed the upcoming visit and meal with worry. The twins were now in the terrible twos stage when it was difficult to keep them from running about the house and wreaking havoc. In fact, their recent antics in their own home had caused him to worry about his sons getting burned by the hot woodstove.

"Dat, Dat!" Jacob squealed. "Cake?"

"I'm sure there will be cake, Jacob, and other desserts as well." He had wanted to contribute to the meal, but his family had insisted that there was no need to bring anything since all the food was taken care of.

Joshua had received the monies from the sale of his farm and buggy a couple of weeks ago. He had deposited the check from the sale of his house back in Illinois after one of his earlier physical therapy appointments, relieved to have the cash needed to reimburse his father for the purchase of his buggy and other items bought on his behalf.

He still had the insurance money he'd received for pain and suffering—and Anna's death—but he refused to touch any of it unless necessary. For some reason, it felt wrong.

When Joshua had brought up paying for the house he lived in to his *dat*, Jonas had refused to take money for it. Dat had moved the house onto the property for his eldest son, his father had informed him. Having Joshua back in New Berne was all his father had ever wanted.

"Besides," his *dat* had said, "if you decide you need a bigger place someday, we can switch houses if you want. But I'm more than happy for you to stay in the one you have. Alta and I are fine with ours."

Joshua drove the short ride to his father's house. Dat had suggested that Joshua join him in the dairy business. Apparently the current hire, Nathaniel Hostetler, their late bishop John's nephew, wanted to purchase his own place, and his father had told Joshua that he could use his help. Joshua was seriously considering his *dat's* offer. Having grown up on the farm, Joshua was no stranger to handling cows and taking care of the chores needed to run the dairy business. And he would be working close to Esther and his children while having a good means of support for his family.

There was another buggy already parked near the barn as he turned onto his father's driveway. Esther's family, he realized. Suddenly, he was eager to get inside. Joshua sent up a silent prayer that the young woman—his bride-to-be—hadn't changed her mind about marrying him.

The fact that he wanted her as his wife this much gave him pause. He'd loved Anna with all the love that he'd had. There was no room in his heart for Esther—and there never would be. He never again wanted to risk experiencing the terrible loss of a loved one. After they wed, he would invite Esther into his home with open arms, but their relationship would be as friends raising his children together—and nothing more.

Esther gathered place settings in the kitchen to set the two large tables in the Millers' great room while her mother mashed potatoes. Her *mam* had brought the cranberry sauce she'd made with fresh berries purchased at Kings General store. Esther had baked apple and pumpkin pies while Linda had made a green bean casserole. Her *mam* had spoken with Alta days earlier about what they could add to the meal.

Fannie was to have come today, but she'd called her father yesterday to tell him that Rose had a fever and that she and David had decided it best if they stay home with their sick little girl. Everyone understood, and Esther thought it a wise choice for her friend. Taking Rose outside in the cold could seriously impact the child's health. Not to mention that the fever could be contagious, and others at the gathering could catch the sickness from her.

"*Hallo!*" Joshua called out as he entered the house with his little ones.

"Esther!" Leah cried when she saw her setting the table.

Turning to catch his youngest daughter's hug just as the child barreled into her, Esther met Joshua's gaze over Leah's head and grinned just as Jacob tugged free from his father's hand and raced to her for some cuddles. She hefted him into her arms with a smile. "How is Jacob today?"

"Es-ter!" he said with a sloppy, toothy grin, and then he babbled something she couldn't understand.

Esther was ready as Joshua's other children vied for her attention.

"*Oll recht* now," Joshua said with a clap of his hands. "You need to give Esther room to breathe."

"What about me?" Alta addressed his children after giving Esther a warm look.

"Grossmammi!" JJ raised his little arms, inviting Alta to pick him up.

Esther didn't mind being crowded by Joshua's young'uns. She soon would be their mother, which thrilled her to no end. She smiled as she noted how much the twins had changed. They were becoming more active with each passing day.

With Magda and Linda assisting, the children were ushered into the great room where two tables had been set up to accommodate everyone. Besides Alta, Jonas and Joshua with his children, Esther's parents and her siblings were here. The only ones who haven't arrived yet were Jonas's twin sons, DJ and Danny. Joshua's sister Sadie lived out of state and wouldn't be there. Fannie had confided that Sadie hadn't even come home for their mom's passing, a fact that surprised Esther.

As if her thoughts of them had made them appear, the back door opened and the two blond twins entered with a burst of sound.

"Let the eating commence!" DJ announced as he came in before Danny.

Danny zeroed in on Esther and rushed to her side with a grin. "Why are you marrying Joshua when you could marry me?" he said with a teasing look toward Joshua.

"She knows who the best *bruder* in our family is," Joshua replied as he went to stand by Esther's side, causing everyone within hearing distance to laugh.

Soon Esther helped place platters of turkey and side dishes on both tables. Alta had baked several loaves of bread, which had been sliced and kept warm, and were now ready for butter. Everyone sat down to enjoy the prepared Thanksgiving feast. She sat at a table with Joshua and Linda and their parents. The rest were at the other table, including their brothers and Joshua's children.

"Now that we are all here together, let us pray," Jonas said. "Heads bowed and hands in our laps."

As the adults offered up silent prayers to *Gott*, the room stayed quiet until the twins' little voices interrupted the stillness.

"Turkey!" Jacob cried.

"Cake!" JJ added.

Jonas lifted his head and grinned at Joshua. "Time to eat," he said with a chuckle. "Our youngest ones are hungry."

Dishes were passed around and everyone took what they wanted. Alta had roasted two turkeys, which was more than enough for all to have multiple servings. Jonas had sliced the turkeys earlier and Esther's mother had helped arrange the meat on platters.

Esther accepted the turkey dish from Joshua. He waited for her to take what she wanted before he forked slices onto his own plate.

"We have much to be thankful for this day," Preacher Jonas said. "Soon Alta and I will have a new *dochter*, while Adam and Lovina will have a new *soohn*. Friends for years, we will all finally be family."

All gazes trained on her and Joshua. Esther smiled and attempted to hide how much being the center of everyone's attention made her nervous. She was surprised when she felt Joshua's hand reach for hers under the table. Her groom-to-be captured her gaze and his smile warmed her, making her feel at ease.

Esther was so caught up in Joshua's brown eyes that she heard just the end of her soon-to-be father-in-law's announcement. "…the wedding will be a week from today."

Her heart gave a thump as she watched for their siblings'

reactions. She noted with pleasure that they all seemed happy for her and Joshua.

"We will be well ready for the ceremony and reception," her mother said, who had been told of the date right after she and Joshua had decided.

Alta passed around the breadbasket. "Fannie has offered to host the ceremony, *schweschter*."

"We'd appreciate that." Her *mam* accepted a bowl of mashed potatoes and added some to her father's plate. "I could use Fannie's help planning the food. I know she has some *gut* recipes."

Jonas nodded. "I'll have her reach out to you."

"*Danki*, that would be *wunderbor*." Her *mam* accepted the green bean casserole and served Adam before herself. "But only when Rose is doing much better."

"I'm sure she'll recover quickly," Joshua's *dat* said as he slathered butter over a slice of Alta's bread. "Joshua, what do you think?"

Her betrothed flashed her a smile before turning to his father. "Esther and I are pleased to have our family's support and understanding." He gave Esther's hand a little squeeze, which went a long way to making her feel special.

Esther glanced toward the other table and started to push back her chair so she could attend to the children.

"They are *oll recht*, Esther," Joshua whispered for her ears alone. "My *bruders* will take care of them." He leaned in closer to her. "Relax. You'll have plenty of time to mother them."

She froze then met his gaze. His expression was warm with understanding. So Esther settled down and decided to enjoy the meal before her. Joshua was right. Soon, she would be a mother to his little ones. That fact that Joshua could read her so easily amazed her. He had been playing the attentive beau, wooing her with his looks and his words.

And just like that, Esther realized that she was in trouble because she knew she was falling for her new husband. A man who wanted to marry her, but had warned her that she'd never have his heart. And she'd known and agreed anyway.

She sent up a silent prayer that all would go well in their marriage and she could accept the conditions of her life with Joshua without suffering too terribly the pain of unrequited love.

Chapter Eleven

Tomorrow Joshua would become her husband.

Esther lay in bed, hoping to fall quickly asleep. She experienced a surge of pleasure that swiftly dissipated as she thought about the changes in her life. Once she was his wife, he would hold her future in his hands. In the Amish community, he would be her boss as well as the head of the household. She believed Joshua would be a good husband. But what if, after a time, he decided their marriage had been a terrible mistake?

I can't think that way.

Her sister lay in the other twin bed, and Esther didn't want Linda to know that she was a little nervous about tomorrow. She took several calming breaths. Everything would be *oll recht*, she thought. Joshua was a loving father, and he'd be a fine husband. He'd been warm and reassuring, as if aware that she needed his support, whenever they'd spent time together.

But brief moments in each other's company couldn't make up for the reality of spending a life together, sharing a house.

Esther tossed and turned, unable to get comfortable, her mind in turmoil. She closed her eyes and prayed to *Gott* for His blessing and guidance. She believed that the Lord had brought her and Joshua together, and the thought gave her peace. She smiled and found herself relaxing enough to release all the tension that had been keeping her awake.

The morning of the wedding came quickly. Joshua stood, dressed and ready, in his father's house, waiting for his twin brothers to come for him. Esther had asked her sister Linda to stand up for her, while he'd decided to have both his brothers, DJ and Danny, as his groomsmen. During the past week, he'd gone through a myriad of emotions, from dealing with grief for his late wife intermingled with a surprising sense of excitement and contentment that soon he would have Esther permanently in his life. The realization about Esther should have upset him, but it didn't. His new wife wouldn't be replacing Anna. He and Esther had agreed that their marriage would be different and for the children.

"Are you *oll recht*, soohn?" his *dat* asked as he entered the kitchen, where Joshua was peering through the window that overlooked the driveway.

He turned to gaze at his father. "I'm fine, Dat."

His *dat* studied him intently. "No regrets?"

Joshua raised his eyebrows. "About Esther?"

"*Ja*." His parent approached until the two of them were only a few feet apart. "Esther is a *wunderbor* young woman who will make you a *gut* wife."

"I know." Joshua smiled. "And *nay*, I haven't any regrets."

"The children—"

"Fannie has them." Since his future mother-in-law had agreed that the ceremony be held at his sister and David's *haus*, his *schweschter* had decided it would be easier for everyone if his children were already there before the wedding began.

Joshua heard a double knock and realized his brothers

had arrived. Through the kitchen window, he recognized DJ in the front seat of their buggy.

Dat opened the door.

"Where is the groom?" Danny entered, his gaze zooming in on Joshua.

"I'm glad you made it on time." Joshua picked up his black wide-brimmed felt hat and settled it on his head. "Dat, are you and Alta going to follow us?"

"*Ja,* we'll be right behind you," Jonas said after he smiled at his wife when she came into the kitchen, ready for the ceremony.

Danny and DJ were quiet during the ride to Fannie's. The twins, who usually teased him about Esther, were serious. As Danny drove onto their sister's driveway, Joshua felt his heart begin to beat hard. He was nervous, he realized. Nervous about whether he was doing the right thing, but mostly afraid that Esther would change her mind before the ceremony.

Danny parked their buggy near the house and the twins jumped out, waiting for him to join them.

"You are wedding a lovely girl, *bruder*," DJ said with sincerity.

Joshua nodded. "*Ja,* I am."

"Treat her right," Danny added.

"I will," he replied. "I promise."

His brother grinned at him then, and the three of them stood a moment as their father arrived and parked close to the barn. They waited for their *dat* and Alta to join them before they approached their sister's house. Fannie opened the door for them, and as they entered, Joshua immediately spotted Esther's family…and then Esther.

Joshua inhaled sharply when he saw her. Wearing a beautiful royal blue dress with a white apron and *kapp*—

traditional Amish wedding apparel—Esther looked beautiful. Golden highlights in her dark blond hair seemed to glow in the sunlight shining through the window. She met his gaze and smiled when she saw him, and he felt this hard, instant kick in his gut. He became unaware of anyone else but her as he watched her approach with glistening green eyes and a warm smile just for him.

"Joshua. Joshua." His father had to call him twice before Joshua realized that his *dat* had spoken. "It's time for the wedding ceremony."

Nodding, Joshua extended his hand toward his bride-to-be. She accepted his invitation, and he felt the warmth of her delicate hand in his grasp. They exchanged smiles as they followed their families into the great room in his sister and brother-in-law's house.

Acknowledging their guests with a brief nod, Joshua escorted Esther to seats in the middle of the first row reserved for the happy couple. He didn't release her hand, enjoying the sensation of their interwoven fingers.

His brothers sat on his left, and Linda sat on Esther's right.

The room was quiet as the church elders rose and took their places in front of the attendees and the happy couple. Joshua was ready for this. He was eager to have Esther permanently in his life and his home.

Esther had been a bit worried as her brother Henry drove her and Linda to Fannie's for her wedding—until Joshua had entered the house. His warm smile made her immediately relax, and she'd felt hopeful and happy…along with a wealth of affection and pleasure that had frequently overwhelmed her whenever she'd envisioned her life with Joshua Miller.

They would make this marriage between them work, she thought. She would be a good wife to Joshua and the best mother she could be to his adorable little ones.

Retaining hold of her hand, Joshua escorted her to their seats. When Bishop David and Joshua's father, Preacher Jonas, moved toward the front of the room, her soon-to-be husband lightly squeezed her fingers in reassurance. Esther smiled at him, ready to marry this handsome man beside her.

"*Willkomm*, Joshua, Esther and their families," the bishop said, his expression solemn. "We are here to witness the joining of this young couple before us. *Gott* has shown that Joshua and Esther's union will be a blessed one." A smile transformed his features. "Let us start with a hymn."

Joshua opened the hymnal that someone had thoughtfully placed below his chair. Her future father-in-law, Jonas, began, and everyone joined in. As she sang, she could hear Joshua's clear masculine voice beside her. Her heart leapt as she glanced in her groom's direction, and he met her gaze with warmth in his brown eyes. Esther knew she had feelings for this man, but what they were suddenly became clear. She sent up a silent prayer asking the Lord that Joshua would care for her one day as someone more than simply a mother for his children.

The hymn was shorter than others sang during Sunday church service. Once it ended, the bishop addressed her and Joshua, speaking about marriage and the blessings of *Gott*'s love. From there, he continued to talk about what was expected from the union and how both would be joined for life. Jonas talked about passages from the Bible, and Esther listened to every word. However, her thoughts remained on Joshua, their hands still joined, fingers entwined.

Finally, Jonas asked his son and his bride to approach

the church elders for the exchange of vows. At that moment, the solemn quiet in the room shattered when a little voice called out. *"Dat!* Est-er!"

Esther glanced toward the children and realized two-year-old Jacob had been the one who had called out. Esther's mother and her aunt Alta quickly shushed him with a gentle finger across his lips and a whisper in his ear, and then did the same with JJ, who had opened his mouth, ready to join in. Amused, Esther fought a smile and saw a flicker of the same expression on Joshua's face before he grew solemn again.

The bishop's lips curved for barely a second before he gazed at her and Joshua without a smile. The occasion was serious and couldn't be taken lightly. "…Are you willing to enter wedlock together as *Gott* in the beginning ordained and commanded?"

Esther looked at Joshua. *"Ja,"* they said together.

"Joshua, are you confident that Esther, our sister, is ordained by *Gott* to be your wedded wife?" the bishop asked. "Will you care for her, never leave her, cherish her and be there for her if she becomes bodily ill?"

There was a heartbeat where Esther feared he would say *"nay."*

"Ja. I will." Joshua spoke clearly and loudly for all to hear, and Esther breathed a sigh of relief.

The bishop then turned to Esther and repeated similar words, but used *Joshua* and *husband* instead.

Esther didn't hesitate in her answer. *"Ja,* I will."

Joshua released her fingers as they faced each other. Then they clasped right hands as the bishop said the words that pronounced them husband and wife. Her new husband nodded but didn't cry, though considering the conditions of their marriage, Esther hadn't expected him to. Jonas and the bishop brushed away tears. Blinking back her own, Esther glimpsed family members wiping their eyes. Emotion was high in the room, but no one congratulated them. The occasion was a solemn one; everyone understood that the marriage would stand until death.

Her mother and Alta quickly left for her parents' house to make sure all was ready for the meal the bride's family would provide the newly wedded couple and their guests. She and her new husband climbed into the buggy that would take them to the reception, which Danny would drive. Linda and Joshua's other brother, their attendants, got in after them, and they were off.

None of their siblings congratulated them on their marriage. The mood was serious, as it usually was after every wedding in the Amish church.

Joshua didn't say a word or attempt to take her hand during the ride. Esther tried not to let it worry her, but considering the type of marriage she had entered, it was hard not to. She shouldn't want him to hold her hand, but she couldn't help it.

When they arrived for the reception, Danny, the driver, got out first and held the door open for everyone to exit the vehicle. Joshua climbed out before Esther and initially offered his hand to help her, but then he quickly released it. They made their way toward the house with their attendants behind them. Esther felt a sudden chill and hugged her arms across her woolen coat. The action must have drawn her groom's attention because suddenly he looked at her. She attempted to assure him that she was fine with a small smile. To her surprise and happiness, Joshua finally reached for her hand and gave it a brief squeeze before letting it go. They entered the house, filled with wondrous, mouthwatering food scents.

"It smells *gut* in here," DJ, her new brother-in-law, said. "I'm starving and could eat a horse."

"That would mean killing animals vital to our way of life," Danny replied dryly.

Esther chuckled. She couldn't help herself because the twins' humorous outburst broke the seriousness of the moment. To her astonishment, she heard Joshua's laughter. She grinned, pleased by the teasing exchange between brothers.

Joshua entered his new in-laws' house, his thoughts centered on his new wife beside him. He'd suffered mixed emotions during the ceremony. Although it was a much simpler one because he was a widower, he'd been unable to stop thinking about when he'd married Anna years ago. It wasn't until he'd sensed Esther's nervousness that he'd focused his attention on his bride-to-be and reached for her hand to reassure her. Esther and he were now man and wife, and they would remain so until death. Once they'd said their vows and were told the union was complete and blessed, it had been difficult for him to imagine it.

He liked Esther, his new bride. He honestly did, but that didn't make his grief for Anna go away. At times, it still had the power to overwhelm him. Joshua had offered Esther a marriage of convenience, and she had accepted. Still, he didn't want her to feel like she didn't belong in his children's lives...in his life. While he would never fall in love with her, he was sure they would be good friends while they raised his children. He knew that what he'd asked of her probably wasn't fair. Joshua had to remind himself that she'd married him because she'd wanted to. *But what if she wants more from me than I'm able to give?*

His brothers made cracks about the delicious scent of the upcoming meal, which made him relax. He looked at his wife, and her amusement was evident in her smile. He could sense any tension within her dissipate. She met his gaze and grinned. "I guess we are hungry about now."

Lovina, his mother-in-law, and her sister Alta, who was also Joshua's stepmother, must have spent hours roasting chickens. Mashed potatoes and multiple vegetable dishes were the perfect sides since Joshua loved all of them.

Since only the bishop and their families were attending, everyone fit into one room in the area called an *Eck*, a U-shaped table arrangement where usually only the newlyweds and their attendants sat. Joshua appreciated that today everything was different, more informal. He could tell that his new bride felt the same by the way she beamed at him once she eyed the table setup and all the food.

Everyone clearly enjoyed the meal. When the main course was done, Fannie, along with Alta and Lovina's help, brought out the desserts. Fannie had insisted on providing a cake and various sweets to tempt any palate. At that point, his children, who sat close to them in the one long part of the table arrangement, moved. Magda and Leah approached with their little brothers. As soon as the twins saw them, they pulled from their sisters' grasps and ran to them. To his surprise, his sons demanded Esther's attention first. She smiled, her expression soft as she lifted them onto her lap, one on each knee.

Magda appeared at Joshua's side. "Sorry, Dat."

Leah's lip quivered as she echoed her older sister. "*Ja,* sorry, Dat."

"What are you apologizing for, *dechter?*" Joshua gazed at his daughters with affection. "You are always *willkomm* to join us." He shifted his chair back and patted his knees. Despite being older, Magda and Leah grinned before they climbed onto his lap, clearly happy to be there.

Esther locked gazes with him, and instinctively, they shared smiles of warm understanding. And Joshua realized he loved this feeling of having a new wife and his children at his side.

When the meal was done, Esther got up as if she would help clean the tables.

"*Nay,*" Linda said. "Not today, schweschter. This is your wedding. Sit and relax until you are ready to leave."

If a newly wedded couple had been both single and never married, they would spend their first night as man and wife in the home of the bride's parents. But because he had been a widower and things were different for him, he, Esther and the children would all return home to begin their life as a family.

Lovina entered the room. "Magda, Leah, please bring your brothers upstairs to your bedrooms for the night."

Esther's mouth gaped open briefly. "But, Mam, they're coming home with us."

"*Nay,* dochter. Tonight is your wedding night, and you will be spending the night alone with your new husband." She nodded approvingly as his children left their laps and obeyed their new grandmother.

Joshua froze for several heartbeats, realizing they would have to go home together alone. The one thing Esther had insisted on with this marriage was that no one other than the two of them would know that theirs wouldn't be a true marriage. He studied his wife, feeling her apprehension, and leaned close to whisper in her ear. "Relax, wife. All will be well."

By the sudden uneasiness in her expression, he knew he hadn't reassured her.

He stood and gently smiled at her. "Let's go home."

Chapter Twelve

Needing to make three trips from the buggy to the house and back, Joshua retrieved massive, heavy cardboard boxes of packed food, amused at his new mother-in-law's insistence that they take it all home. Setting the last of them on the table, he opened the first box. Everything inside was covered with foil. By the smell emanating past the wrapping, he knew that this held packets of roast chicken. Finding space in the refrigerator, he placed all the chicken on the bottom shelf. When he was done, he returned to see what was inside the second box. As he was taking stock of its contents, Esther entered the room with a smile, which he noticed when he glanced over his shoulder at her.

"Do you need help?" She moved to stand beside him. "What's in this one? I see you already emptied one of them. Because of the familiar smell, I can tell it had chicken in it." She sighed. "Did my *mam* think we could actually fit all of this in the refrigerator?"

He detected the sweet scent of her, as he had when he held her earlier. She smelled of vanilla and black cherry. Joshua wasn't sure if it was her natural aroma or if the pleasant smell came from her shampoo. "We'll manage. All this food will come in handy once our children return tomorrow." He studied the second box's contents and saw dishes covered with plastic wrap and others with foil. "Vegetables. Not sure what the others are." He lifted the foil on one dish. "Mashed potatoes." He flashed her a grin. "I love mashed potatoes."

Esther grinned at him. "*Gut* to know."

With his new wife's assistance, he found a place in the refrigerator for more food. The last big box held multiple desserts, including a large section of cake covered by a clear plastic lid dome.

Once she saw the cake, Esther picked up the covered plate. "This will go fine with our tea." She bit her lip. "Unless you want coffee."

He shook his head. "Tea and cake sound perfect." And he was rewarded by her grin.

It had been an emotional day. At times, he'd struggled with thoughts of Anna, and then at others, he felt at peace as he reminded himself that his decision to marry Esther because of the children was a good one. The fact that he genuinely liked her made everything much better. Yet when he watched her light the stove and put the kettle on to heat, his mind filled with the image of Anna doing the same thing. And it hurt. A lot.

It was December 4. He and Esther had a long winter ahead of them. It could be a tough time for many, like it had been for Anna, who had become melancholy over the frigid winter months. Would Esther be the same way? He hoped not. But then he immediately felt guilty for recalling something his beloved Anna had suffered from through no fault of her own. There had been times it had been difficult for her to care for the children, and he'd had to step in. Not that he minded spending time with his little ones. It had given him experience in caring for them after their mother's death, which had left the five of them to cope alone.

The kettle whistled, and Esther took it off the flame. He watched her move efficiently as she poured two cups of hot water and placed a tea bag in each one. Then, beaming at him, she carried the tea to the table, returning to the counter to get sugar and then grab milk from the refrigerator. She set both close to his cup, then went back for plates with two good-sized pieces of chocolate cake, one for each of them. She was grinning as she gave him his snack and took the seat next to him.

Something about her good humor and the way she moved about his kitchen, clearly at home in it, eased back his grief. Joshua could only enjoy his new wife and their first "meal" alone together.

"Christmas is in a few weeks," he commented, interrupting their comfortable silence.

Esther swallowed her sip of tea. "*Ja,* I've already been working on gifts for your children."

"*Our* children," he said.

"Our children," she corrected with a wide smile.

Joshua was impressed. Esther was a highly capable young woman. "Do you know what you want for Christmas?"

She shook her head, but he noted the soft blush on her pretty cheeks. "*Nay,* you have already given me a gift. You opened your home to me and gave me your children to mother and cuddle."

He made the decision right then that he would find the best gift for his new wife, perhaps with help from his family if needed. But he had a feeling he would figure it out on his own, for Esther was open and giving. And he would enjoy learning every little thing about her.

They sipped the tea and enjoyed the cake. "What did you do for a living back in Illinois?" Esther asked as she forked another bite of chocolate cake.

"I was a farmer. I grew crops and had livestock."

Esther looked impressed. "Did you have cows like your *dat*?"

"I did. In fact, I've decided to join my *vadder* in his dairy business." He watched her lick chocolate frosting from her bottom lip. "I told you about it a couple of weeks ago. What I didn't tell you was that I grew up on Dat's dairy farm. I know the work so it will be an easy transition for me. Apparently, Nathaniel, the young man who is currently helping him, hopes to be ready to buy a place of his own soon." He drank from his cup of tea. "Until then, the three of us will work well together, especially caring for the stock and completing the chores that need to be done during the winter months."

"That sounds like a fine plan." She stood. "Would you like more cake?"

"I better not."

She smirked at him, and he found her adorable. "It's our wedding day and our *kinner* aren't here. If any time was a *gut* time to have some, it's today. Now."

He laughed. "*Okey.* I'll have another piece then."

With a look of approval, she picked up his plate then sliced him another piece at the counter. "More tea?" she asked as she brought back his dish.

"*Ja.*" This time with her was nice, Joshua thought. It was almost like they had just met and found pleasure in each other's company.

The water was still hot, as confirmed when she lit the burner, and within seconds on the flame, the kettle whistled. She refilled their cups and brought over fresh tea bags. As she approached, the sun shone through the kitchen window, highlighting her blond locks. Soon it would be dark, and he had a feeling that something would change between them. Joshua gazed at her intently as she resumed her seat.

"I have a question for you." Joshua fixed his tea the way he preferred it.

She smiled at him. "And what is that?"

"My *dat* told me you used to have a cleaning business. It's obvious by how well you've taken care of this *haus* that you were excellent at it." He ate a forkful of cake. "What made you give it up?"

She drew a sharp breath before she released it. "It didn't work out. I found working with clients had become stressful after word spread and I was hired by more *Englishers*." Esther sipped from her tea. "I was already working part-time for Fannie. She needed more employees once she decided to add a catering business to the services offered by her restaurant." She smiled. "I was happy she hired me full-time."

"And you like working for her," he said, watching his new wife carefully.

Esther flashed him a smile. "I do. I love cooking and waiting on people. It helps that Fannie is ready to step in whenever I encounter a difficult customer."

Joshua laughed. "*Ja,* she can be fierce when she needs to be."

She nodded. "But she is kind about it, and even the most trying customers are happy with her and the luncheonette by the time they leave."

After lingering at the kitchen table for a time, Joshua stood and held out his hand to his new wife. "Would you care to sit in our living room?"

"*Ja,* I would, husband," she teased as she accepted his help to stand.

And the two of them relaxed together on the sofa in the other room. For the remainder of the evening, they enjoyed the warmth from the woodstove as they continued to learn more about each other.

* * *

Joshua arose the next morning and got ready for the day. He was glad that his little ones weren't due back for a while so he could enjoy a leisurely breakfast with Esther. With the woodstove emitting heat after he'd added two logs, he went into the kitchen to put on the coffeepot. It was a routine he'd gotten used to since he'd moved in…only it was a lot easier to manage now that his legs were strong again.

He was surprised by how quickly the physical therapy had helped him. When he'd mentioned his astonishment to the technician, the young man had told him the reason for his quick recovery was because he had been putting pressure on both legs while using his walker. If he'd realized how well he could have improved with physical therapy, he would have gone sooner. The doctors who had taken care of him in Arthur hadn't once mentioned that physical therapy was needed. *Thank you, Lord, for Dr. Ramsey and the doctor's insight and quick response to my pain and never-ending weakness.*

It was still early. The sun had yet to rise. Joshua stood at the kitchen window, peering into the hint of light in the dawn sky.

"*Gut* morning." Esther entered the room, dressed and smiling. She had rolled and neatly pinned her dark blond hair. Her prayer *kapp* was white with a crispness that suggested that it might be new. The vivid purple color of her dress somehow matched and enhanced the unusual green shade of her pretty eyes. "Coffee?" he asked.

"*Ja, danki,* but you don't have to wait on me." She brought milk and sugar to the table. "Would you like breakfast? I can make eggs and sausage and bacon if you'd like."

"Not yet." He softened his words. "How about we sit and enjoy the moment together? If we're ever to get a brief respite from the children—our children—we should enjoy it. Take any moment we can just to sit and relax in the early hours of the morning like this." Joshua saw emotion play across her face when he'd referred to his children as theirs. And it was true, for they were now man and wife, and she would be a mother to his little ones for the rest of their lives.

Esther fixed her coffee and then, as he'd suggested, enjoyed the quiet time to drink it. "Do you think our *kinner* are upset that we married?" she asked, surprising him.

Joshua frowned as he locked gazes with her. "They love you. Why would they be upset?"

"I know they have always been happy whenever they saw me, but living here...taking the place of their *mudder*?" The furrow on her forehead told him how concerned she was about this.

"The twins couldn't possibly remember Anna," he said, and then questioned whether he should have mentioned his late wife's name when he witnessed anxiety enter her expression.

"But Magda and Leah...they must remember her well." Esther took a sip from her mug as if she wanted to hide her thoughts.

"They will be fine," he assured her. "It's been easy to see how much they care for you."

Drawing a sharp breath, Esther set down her coffee. "Magda seemed overly quiet after the wedding. She didn't say a word before she went upstairs, as my *mam* asked, to choose a bed to sleep in."

Did Magda have a problem with his new wife? Joshua wondered. He hoped not. There was nothing he could do at present until the children returned, and then he could talk with her.

The sun brightened the morning sky a while later. Joshua

didn't know how long they'd been sitting together quietly, drinking coffee. He knew he'd had at least three cups. Esther seemed to sip from hers more slowly. Finally, she stood. "Breakfast?"

He nodded. "Eggs and sausage are fine. But then so is cereal. I don't want you to fuss on your first day as my wife."

Smiling, Esther moved to the stove. "I can make pancakes—and there are muffins and Danish that my *mam* sent home with us."

Joshua grinned at her. "Muffins and Danish sound *gut* to me." He was glad that she took his words to heart. Esther needed to enjoy the less active times when their children were absent. Esther would soon be a busy wife and mother. He didn't need her to cook him breakfast this morning. And they could certainly find something for lunch in that huge supply of food his new in-laws had insisted they take home.

Lunch came and went, and for the midday meal he and Esther had enjoyed chicken salad sandwiches, which his new wife made from one of the roasted chickens after she'd convinced him that the work was easy and quickly accomplished. After he heard a commotion on his back step, Joshua felt prepared when his children burst into the house with his in-laws.

"Dat!" Magda cried, running to wrap her arms about his waist.

"Dat!" Leah followed her sister and hugged him tightly.

Lovina held JJ while Adam carried Jacob. "Dat! Dat!" both cried in unison as they struggled to get down from their new grandparents' arms.

Esther had gone into the children's rooms to make sure everything was as it should be before they came home. Upon hearing the noise, she entered the kitchen with a soft, affectionate smile for his young'uns. "Esther!" Leah ran to hug her before stepping aside as Jacob and JJ clamored to get their new mother's hugs. Magda—his eldest child—stayed back, he noticed.

"*Hallo,* Dat, Mam," Esther said as she smiled at Leah who reached for her again after her sons ran to her parents.

"*Dochter.*" Her father grinned as he lifted JJ. "*Soohn.*"

"They were *wunderbor,* well-behaved *kinner,*" her mother assured them as she picked up Jacob and gazed happily at the little boy in her arms.

"*Gut,* I'm glad to hear that." Joshua watched his in-laws with approval. "The twins can be a handful."

Lovina laughed. "We had lots of help. Linda was there, but it was my *soohns* who stepped up to entertain them."

"Magda, did you have a *gut* time with my *eldre*?" Esther asked as she held her youngest daughter close before releasing her.

The little girl glanced toward her new grandparents and nodded. "*Ja.*"

Esther caught his gaze, her green eyes a mirror for her thoughts. She looked sad and worried.

"Magda, aren't you going to say *hallo* to Esther?" Joshua recognized the sudden spike in his wife's anxiety when he asked, based on how her brow furrowed and her spine stiffened. His daughter's behavior had changed drastically since he and Esther had taken their wedding vows.

Magda looked at Esther but didn't smile. "*Hallo.*"

"I'm glad you had fun," his wife murmured.

"We're going to head out," his new father-in-law said as he handed JJ to Joshua. "I hope you'll let them stay with us again."

Joshua nodded as his son snuggled sleepily against his shoulder. "*Ja,* of course. We appreciate you taking care of them for us."

"We enjoyed having them," Lovina assured him with a sweet expression that told him how much Esther's parents already cared for their new *kins kind.* The woman smiled at her daughter as she set Jacob down and watched him run to Magda. "Don't be a stranger before the Christmas holidays."

"I won't," Esther replied with a smile.

Joshua could tell his new wife wasn't her normal happy self, although she managed to hide it well from her *mam* and *dat.*

After their children thanked Adam and Lovina for allowing them to spend the night, Esther followed her parents to the door. He watched as her mother whispered something in his new wife's ear, which caused Esther to grin—a genuine grin that gave him hope. Whatever Lovina had said seemed to ease his new bride's concern.

When she returned after waving to her parents as they left, Esther looked about the room and realized that it was empty of children. Her shoulders slumped, and her good humor seemed to fade. "They're in their room," he told her, and she managed a small smile that confirmed how upset she was.

Joshua couldn't help being concerned about Magda's behavior and how it would greatly affect Esther's happiness if his daughter refused to accept her. "Don't worry. There will be a few adjustments in our family now that we're married. Everything will be fine soon."

"I hope so," he heard Esther murmur beneath her breath, and he decided right then that he would do all he could to help ease her into this new life she'd agreed to.

Even if things get tougher before they improve.

Chapter Thirteen

❧

Esther grew more concerned when Magda continued to be withdrawn from her. To everyone else in the family, she was the happy little girl that Esther had known before she and Joshua had wed. Prior to yesterday's ceremony, she and her husband's eldest child had gotten along well. But something had changed drastically in Magda's eyes. And she had no idea what to do about it.

After a simple supper of soup and grilled cheese sandwiches, they all sat in the living room except the twins, whom Esther, with Joshua's assistance, had tucked into bed not long after their meal. She'd taken the chair next to her new husband and mended Leah's dress where the hem had come undone. At first, she'd thought the evening would show an improvement in Magda but the child excused herself after only a half hour in their company, urging her sister to follow. The girl murmured goodnight to her father without meeting Esther's gaze. Leah smiled warmly before she gave goodnight hugs to her and Joshua.

Alone with Joshua now, she sighed as she faced him. "Magda is upset with me. Has been since yesterday." Esther thought the child might be missing her *mam*. It couldn't be easy for the six-year-old to accept another woman in her late mother's place.

Joshua, who had been reading the current issue of *The Budget*, looked up from the Amish newspaper to meet her gaze. "This is all new to her. She'll come around." He folded the newspaper and put it aside. "She's always loved you. Don't give up on her."

"I'd never give up on her or any of the children!" She gasped, horrified that he thought she could. "I love every one of them."

Her husband regarded her with a soft expression. "I'll have a talk with her."

Esther shook her head. "*Nay*, please wait. Maybe it will help if I find something for us to do together."

Joshua smiled. "That sounds like a *wunderbor* idea."

"We could make cookies, but I'm thinking it might be better if we do something away from the *haus*." Esther gave it some thought and recalled how much she had liked it when her mother showed her how to sew. "What if I could teach her how to use my *mam*'s sewing machine?" It seemed like a good idea, but what if it didn't work?

"I think sewing together may remind her how much she enjoyed spending time with you. And how much she loves you," he said, approving her plan. "And maybe she'll tell you why she's been upset." He stood and held out his hand. "Come into the kitchen."

Placing the dress she'd mended over the arm of her chair, Esther accepted Joshua's help to rise and followed him into the other room. "How do I convince her to come with me?"

"Simply ask. I don't think she'll say *nay*." Her husband pulled out a chair for her at the table and she automatically sat down. "Magda had fun staying with your *eldre*."

Anxious, Esther sprang from her seat, unable to sit still. "I should let my *mudder* know we're coming." She began to pace from one end of the kitchen to the other.

"I doubt that's necessary." Joshua stood and eased her back onto her chair. "Sit and relax for a while. You'll figure it out." He put water to heat in the kettle. "Adam and Lovina sounded eager to have our *kinner* stay with them again."

She gaped at him in surprise. "You're making us tea?"

He chuckled. "I told you I can handle coffee. Did you think tea is more difficult for me to make?"

"*Nay,* but I thought—"

"You're not a servant in this *haus*, Esther. I will assist wherever I can." Joshua took two cups down from the cabinet and added a tea bag to each one. He brought their cups to the table. "I start work with my *vadder* soon and won't be around as much. Let me do what I can when I'm home."

"I didn't expect you to help me, husband." She offered him a genuine smile. "You're a *gut* man, Joshua Miller."

Joshua took a sip of his tea without responding. The long-drawn-out silence that followed when he didn't look at her became uncomfortable for Esther.

Finally, he met her gaze. "We're friends raising children together. You won't be doing this alone."

She was aware of the conditions of their marriage. Yet his comment that they were friends still hurt. As a young girl, she'd always longed for a strong relationship with the man she'd hoped to marry one day. Esther knew she should be grateful that she now had a family. And she was, but she couldn't help praying for more. While she knew Joshua was trying to reassure her, she instead felt the division between her and her husband widen. *It will be fine. I knew what I was getting into. He made the terms of the marriage clear when he proposed before I chose to marry him. I will be happy because I have his respect and his children to mother.*

Her love for the children brought back the dilemma she

had with Magda. Should she give her mother a call? It wasn't an emergency, although to her it felt like one because of the sudden change in the child's behavior toward her.

Her husband pushed the sugar bowl in her direction. "What are you contemplating so hard, wife?"

"Whether or not I should call my *mam* to ask if I can use her sewing room tomorrow. I know she's awake." After adding sugar to her cup, Esther took a tentative taste of her tea and hummed with appreciation. "While Mam would never say *nay*, I'd feel better knowing that she's expecting us."

He studied her thoughtfully. "What are you going to tell her?"

Esther nibbled nervously on her bottom lip. "The truth."

"Then you'd better call her now before it gets too late." Joshua smiled with understanding.

"I need my phone." She shoved back her chair.

"Slowly. Calmly," her husband advised. "I don't want you to fall in your haste."

She blushed. "*Recht.*" Fighting the urge to rush for her phone, she took two steps then faced Joshua. "*Danki,*" she whispered with tears in her eyes.

His expression softened. "You have nothing to thank me for, Esther. It's me who must thank you for being my wife."

She grinned at him before she left to get her phone.

"We're here!" Esther called out as she entered her parents' home with Magda the next morning.

Her mother came into the kitchen from a back room. "*Hallo!*" She hugged Magda and then Esther. "*Willkomm!*" She focused her attention on the six-year-old. "Magda, I hear my *dochter* is going to teach you how to sew. How exciting! I did the same for Esther, and now she is a *wunderbor* seamstress."

Magda shot Esther a quick glance. "You did?"

"*Ja,* I did. And now my Esther will do the same for you." Her *mam* leaned over and whispered, "And when you're done? We'll have milk and cookies. What do you think of that?"

Her new daughter grinned. "I think that would be delicious!"

Esther was relieved to see Magda's return to the precious, good-natured child she'd known before she married her father. She was glad she'd explained the situation to her mother, who was winning over Magda with kindness and the promise of sweet treats with milk.

"Why don't you two go upstairs and get started?" her mother suggested. "There are leftover remnants of fabric you can use. I have no need of them and planned to give them away anyway."

"*Danki,* Mam." She smiled at her mother. "Come with me, Magda." Esther desperately wanted to call the little girl *daughter* but she didn't want to push or prevent any hope of their relationship improving with their time together.

Esther allowed Magda to precede her upstairs. Her daughter seemed to know which direction the sewing room was, probably from when she'd spent the night here after the wedding. The child turned toward the right in the hallway but waited for Esther to open the door and gesture for her to step inside.

"Let's see what fabric your *grossmammi* left for us, *ja*?" Esther smiled as she faced Magda. Her spirits fell when she saw the six-year-old's closed-off expression. She tried to remain bright and cheery. "Pick out a color. What would you like to make?"

"Can we make a pot holder for Grossmammi Lovina?" Magda said, surprising her.

"*Ja*, of course we can. I'm sure my *mudder* will love that." She waited patiently as her daughter went through the brightly colored folded remnants to see which one she wanted.

"I like these." Magda held up two different solid pieces of fabric—a light green and a forest green.

"Those will be fine," Esther assured her. She found hope that Magda seemed pleased by her approval. "Shall we make one side light and the other dark? And which color should we use to trim it? The forest green? We can make the hanging loop the same color."

"*Ja*, that sounds *gut*." Magda held the material tightly against her and refused to let go when Esther reached for it.

"Let me show you how it works, *ja*?" Esther grabbed two solid colors of blue then pulled a chair up to the treadle sewing machine. "First, we'll need thread to match our material." She found the blue and threaded it through the machine and needle. "Next, we'll cut out a fabric square of each color, one for each side of the batting which provides the padding for the pot holder to keep hands and fingers from getting burned."

Esther showed Magda how the bottom foot pedal worked the machine by pressing it with her foot. She taught her about how the needle moved thread in an up-and-down motion through the fabric to stitch it together. Esther made the blue pot holder for Alta, her aunt. Magda did a good job guiding fabric through the machine under Esther's watchful eye to make the green potholder for Esther's mother. Magda was too short to work the treadle, but with Esther's help, she was able to sew neat, even stitches. While they worked together, Magda seemed to be her normal happy self. It wasn't until they were finished that the child's sullenness toward Esther returned.

"We can give these to my mother and aunt for Christmas," Esther said.

Magda nodded without a word.

Esther held in a sigh. "Shall we put these in a bag and then head downstairs for our cookies and milk?"

"*Okey,*" the child said, finally talking, even if it was only one word.

Her mother kept the conversation going as she served cookies and milk. While she was glad Magda enjoyed her *mam*'s company, Esther couldn't help feeling saddened by the loss of the child's affection.

By the time they got home a half hour before lunch, Esther felt discouraged and tired. As she drove past the house to park the buggy near the barn, she was suffering from cramps. She waited for Magda to head inside before she followed. Once in the house, she immediately found the bottle of acetaminophen and took two with a glass of water. Joshua was nowhere in sight, which was just as well, for she didn't want him to worry. She heard Magda calling for her father as Esther took a seat and lay her head on the surface of the kitchen table.

"What's wrong?"

Esther lifted her head to meet her husband's concerned gaze.

"I'm fine. Just some cramps. I took something for them." She managed a smile. "They'll go away eventually." She shifted back on her chair. "You talked with Magda?"

The worry remained in his expression as he sat next to her. "*Ja,* she seems excited about the pot holder she made."

"I'm glad." She held her abdomen and tried not to grimace. "She learns quickly. I watched her carefully." She managed a chuckle. "She couldn't reach the treadle so I did that part for her, but she guided the fabric and chose the colors." Esther repositioned her body to ease the pain, but she got no relief.

"So, teaching her worked." Joshua continued to study her. "She seems happy."

"We had milk and cookies before we left." She swallowed hard and fought tears. "My *mam's* idea. She loves my *mudder*."

"You're hurting," her husband burst out. "What can I do to help?"

"I don't know if there is anything you can do." Esther blinked rapidly. "I get these sometimes. I just have to struggle through them."

"Dat!" Magda exclaimed as she bolted into the room. "Can we eat lunch soon?"

Joshua pulled his worried gaze from his wife. She looked terrible. Her skin was paler than usual, though she was trying to hide the fact that she was upset and fighting tears. He glanced toward his daughter. "We'll eat in a little bit. I heard you had cookies and milk, so you should be able to wait until it's ready."

Magda nodded and spun around, ready to hurry from the room.

"Magda," he called.

She faced him. "*Ja,* Dat?"

"Did you have a *gut* time today sewing with Esther?" He watched her reaction carefully.

His eldest shrugged. "It was *okey.* I learned a lot and got to make the pot holder." She paused. "I like Gross-mammi Lovina."

"That's *gut.*" He cast a look toward his wife and saw sadness that told him as much as Magda's answers about her day. "I'll call you when lunch is ready." He reached out to place a hand on Esther's shoulder. "She hasn't warmed to you. I would have thought with the morning you spent together that she would have." He squeezed her shoulder lightly before he released her. He stood. "I'm going to have a talk with her."

"*Nay*, please," Esther pleaded. "Let me be the one who speaks with her. *Please*."

He eyed her thoughtfully. "*Okey*. But if you need me to step in, let me know." He stood. "I'm going to add wood to the fire. The temperature is supposed to drop considerably."

"Joshua." Her soft voice drew his attention as he started toward the other room. She drew in a sharp breath as he faced her. "I won't give up on her. Once I find out what's bothering her, I'll be able to do something about it." She bent her head as she pressed her hands over her lower stomach. "I love your children."

"*Our* children," he insisted. Joshua studied her a long moment and saw that she was still suffering from cramps. He recalled how much his legs had hurt him after the accident and how he'd feared that his pain would never go away. Were her cramps a sign that there was something physically seriously wrong with her? But if she knew why she suffered, wouldn't she have told him? There had to be something he could do to ease her pain. But what? Whatever medicine she had taken didn't seem to be helping her. He could make lunch, though. At least that was something he could do.

Chapter Fourteen

Joshua sat in a chair in the living room later that night. "Are you *oll recht*?"

Esther nodded. "I'm feeling much better. It was a *gut* afternoon. And tomorrow will be a better one."

"Have you talked with Magda?" He put his feet up on an ottoman.

"Not yet. I'm trying to figure out the *recht* thing to say." Esther was seated in the chair next to him with her feet up on the matching ottoman. The children were in their beds, and the quiet with her husband by her side was peaceful, soothing to her anxiety about Magda.

"I have faith in you. She'll come around," he assured her. "You're a natural *mudder*. I think she needs to believe that she will always have a place with us, that you won't leave like her—"

"Mam did?" she finished for him.

"*Ja*. Her death was not only hard on me but on the girls, too. The boys don't remember her since they were a year and a half when she died, but I still think they were affected." He tilted his head back and stared at the ceiling. "I still wonder if it was fair for me to propose to you the way I did." Joshua released a weary breath. "You deserve more than I offered you."

Esther was quiet a long time, as if deciding how best to reply. "I knew what I was doing when I married you, Joshua. Everything will be *oll recht*." She shifted her legs on the ottoman. "I am happy to be here. Please don't concern yourself with worry. I'm fine, and pleased to mother your children."

"*Danki*," he said softly.

"No reason to thank me, Joshua. You've accepted me in your home and given me a family. I appreciate how difficult this must be for you and your little ones."

"Our little ones," he said, and her soft laughter made him grin. But then his good humor faded. If he wasn't grieving Anna, he could give Esther a better life than the one they had prearranged. Guilt over taking Esther as his wife hit him hard, reminding him that it would be a long time, if ever, before he would get over Anna's demise.

They sat in silence for a time and Joshua felt himself relaxing. He didn't realize he'd fallen asleep in the chair until a noise disturbed him, and he found himself slouched in his chair in the dark. He heard it again and sat upright, startled to discover the sound was Esther whimpering. He sensed her restless movements. Concerned, needing to see her, he switched on his battery-operated lantern. Keeping the bright light directed away from her face, he studied his wife and saw her face contort with pain as she moaned.

"Esther," he whispered, "you're in pain. How can I help?"

She lay on her side, curled into a ball against the chair seat cushion. "I'll be *okey*."

"*Frau*." His voice was firm and questioning. "Do you have cramps again?"

"*Ja*," she gasped and then groaned. "Bad ones."

"Where is your medicine?" Joshua understood that some

women suffered greatly during their cycle. He decided that Esther's was the reason for her distress.

It took a moment but then she continued. "There's a bottle of pain reliever on the bottom shelf in the cabinet to the right of the sink. It's been long enough for me to take it again."

"I'll get it and a glass of water." He felt great sympathy for her suffering.

Joshua padded in his black-stocking feet into the kitchen where he filled a glass at the sink. Checking where Esther had instructed him to look, he found her bottle of acetaminophen and shook out two pills before returning to her side.

"Here," he said as he handed her the two pills and water. "Let me help you sit up so that you don't choke. Two is the correct amount, *ja*?"

"*Ja, danki*." Her reply was weak. He watched her carefully as she popped the pain relievers into her mouth and washed them down with water.

"You're *willkomm*." He took the water glass and set it on top of a small table on the other side of the room. Joshua hated feeling helpless in the face of her pain. "Does heat help?"

"Sometimes. Not always but I have used it in the past." Esther eased herself back against the chair.

"I'll be right back." Joshua retrieved a hot-water bottle from the linen chest in the corner of the living room. He returned to the kitchen and filled it with hot water after running the faucet for a while to make sure it was hot enough.

His wife's eyes were closed when he returned. He wondered if she'd fallen asleep, but as soon as he approached, she opened them. "Here." He held up the hot-water bottle. "Let's see if this helps."

Joshua handed it to her and watched as she placed it over her lower belly.

"This is thoughtful, Joshua." She shut her eyes briefly and he could tell that she was trying to even and slow her breathing. "*Danki.*" Esther winced and then shifted the source of heat to another area on her abdomen.

"Let me know if you need anything. I'll be right here." He knew Esther wouldn't move from her position so he got comfortable again on his chair. "Our little ones will sleep in."

"You don't have to stay here," Esther said, her voice low. "I'll be *okey.*"

"I'm not going anywhere, *frau.* Try to get some sleep." He closed his eyes and attempted to banish the image of Esther suffering as he tried to go back to sleep. But he couldn't. Joshua wished there was more he could do for her. He forced himself to think about Anna instead of his wife in name only, but it didn't work. The only woman in his thoughts was Esther.

Sounds of the children in their bedrooms woke him up the next morning. Peeking over toward his wife, he was pleased to see that she still slept. At some point, the pills and heat must have eased her pain enough for her to fall asleep and continue to rest this morning.

He got up and checked on the girls first. They were out of bed and playing on the floor with puzzles, with their dolls by their sides. "Would you like breakfast?"

Leah grinned. "I'm hungry. Can we have Esther's pancakes?"

"Not today, dochter," he said with a soft smile. "Esther is feeling a little under the weather."

"What's wrong with her?" Magda, he saw, had perked up at the news. "Is she still sleeping?"

Joshua nodded. "She's in the living room, so you need to be quiet on your way to the kitchen. I thought I'd make her some tea in a little bit. Would you take it to her once I do?" He was surprised when Magda agreed.

After a quick peek at the boys, who thankfully continued to sleep, he led his daughters through the living room to the kitchen, with a finger held over his lips to remind them how quiet they needed to be. He put on the kettle and checked on Esther, who had her eyes closed but was beginning to stir. Joshua then fixed his wife's tea the way he knew she liked it.

"I'll bring it to her," Magda said when the tea was done.

Joshua smiled at his eldest. "*Gut. Danki.* We can have muffins for breakfast. You may eat some cereal first if you'd like."

"I like muffins," Leah said as she accepted the paper plates that he held out to her.

"I'll take this to Esther and be back to help." Magda took careful hold of the cup and carried it to Esther in the living room.

Esther sensed someone in the room before she opened her eyes. Immediately she saw it was daylight by the light filtering through the living room curtains. When she turned to greet her husband with a good morning wish, she was surprised to see Magda cautiously approach where she sat, her footsteps slow as she carried a steaming cup.

"I brought you some tea," the six-year-old said. "*Dat* said you weren't feeling well."

Esther smiled at her warmly as she shifted higher in the chair. "*Danki,* Magda." She accepted the tea and then gestured toward the chair next to hers. "Sit down. There is something I'd like to say."

Magda seemed hesitant to obey.

"It's nothing bad, I promise. I just need to tell you something important."

Esther watched as the tension eased from the girl's shoulders, and was pleased when Magda took the seat. She nodded with approval. "First, I want to assure you that I'm not here to take the place of your *mudder*. I know you loved her. She will always have a special place in your heart, and I don't want to change that."

She studied Magda, comforted when the child nodded as if she understood. "Second, I am fine. I don't plan on going anywhere in case you've been worried about that. I like being here to take care of you and your *schweschter* and *bruders*. I like you and want to be there for you whenever you need me." Esther waited patiently for the girl's response. "Do you understand what I'm saying?"

Her eyes glistening with tears, Magda bit her lip. "*Ja.*"

Esther grinned. "*Gut.* Now give me a few minutes to drink my tea, and then I'll make pancakes for you."

The child regarded her impishly. "Dat said no pancakes today. We're having muffins."

"I like muffins. They sound delicious." Esther leaned closer to her and whispered, "I'll make us pancakes tomorrow."

Magda laughed loudly. "Pancakes tomorrow."

Esther drank her tea while Magda went to tell her father that she would join them for breakfast soon. She was glad she'd had a chance to talk with her daughter. She realized that Magda hadn't been concerned about Esther taking her mother's place. The child had simply been worried that something bad would happen to her like it had her *mam*.

The girls were at the table with buttered muffins on

paper plates when she entered the kitchen. Joshua turned as if he'd sensed her presence.

"*Gut mariga,* husband," she greeted him with a smile, then held up the empty cup. "I appreciate the tea." She looked at Magda. "And I appreciate you bringing it to me. I am a blessed woman with such thoughtful ones taking care of me."

Magda laughed. "We will always take care of you as you do for us."

Joshua's gaze met hers as she turned. Esther rewarded him with a look of pleasure, letting him know that all was fine between her and his oldest daughter.

A hard thump followed by crying at the back of the house had Esther racing toward the twins' bedroom. JJ had managed to climb out of his crib. He'd hit the floor hard and was wailing as he rubbed his right arm and leg. "I fall-ded," he said as she reached down to lift him.

Jacob stood on his mattress, looking as if he was deciding whether to join his brother on the floor. The last thing Esther wanted was for Jacob to get hurt, too.

Joshua had rushed in on Esther's heels. Interpreting the situation correctly, he moved toward Jacob's crib.

Hugging JJ, Esther turned to her husband. "I think they've outgrown their cribs."

"I agree," he said before he grabbed Jacob as the boy swung his leg up, as if to throw himself over the crib railing.

Magda and Leah stood in the doorway with worried frowns.

"They are fine." Joshua shifted his hold on Jacob. "Let's eat breakfast. I'm hungry."

"I am, too," Esther said, and all the children chimed in that they wanted food, too. She was glad she felt much better this morning. The pain could come back once her monthly cycle hit, but she would stay on top of it if she could. Pain reliever and heat were the best relief usually. She'd been stunned—in a good way—when Joshua had prepared a hot-water bottle for her. She knew stress could cause flare-ups. The night's cramps could be related to her new life… and her concern over Magda's earlier behavior. She was pleasantly surprised she'd been able to sleep in the chair.

Days one and two of her married life were complete. She wondered what tomorrow would bring. There was a lot of work to be done in preparation for Christmas. Esther decided to focus on that, the children, the house…and making Joshua happy that he'd married her.

If I can.

No matter what, she intended to enjoy life with her new family.

Chapter Fifteen

"So today we're going to make cupcakes," she said as she smiled at Magda and Leah, who stood next to her at the kitchen table. Esther was using it as a workstation so that her daughters could reach.

A week had passed since their wedding, and Esther had settled into her new life as Joshua's wife and a mother to his children.

"What kind of cupcakes?" Leah asked.

Esther smiled. "I thought we'd bake two flavors—chocolate and vanilla."

The child nodded approvingly. "Dat loves chocolate."

"*Ja*, he does." She'd placed the ingredients they would need on the table close to the large mixing bowl they would be using. "Eggs first." She opened the carton. "Each of you take one."

Magda looked worried as she obeyed. "What if we get eggshells in the bowl?"

"Then we'll take them out. That's why we put the eggs in first." Esther continued to instruct them on cake-making and watched, hiding her amusement, as each girl carefully completed her assigned task. After they had made two flavors of batter, which were poured into separate cupcake pans, she encouraged the girls to play in the living room until the baking was done.

"I'll call you when they're ready," she promised. The sisters wanted to watch as Esther pulled the baked cupcakes from the oven.

In the ensuing quiet, Esther reflected on how well life was going for her and her new family. The twins were currently taking their midmorning naps. Joshua had gone to work at Jonas's dairy farm starting this past Monday. She and Joshua had established a routine of waking up early together with Esther preparing the two of them a hearty breakfast that would hold them until lunch. Joshua returned for the midday meal and a few hours at home before he went back to the dairy farm to finish his chores.

Christmas was less than two weeks away. Whenever she had a quiet moment, she continued to work on gifts for Joshua and their little ones, which was difficult considering they had four active children. She'd been working on matching scarves for her husband and sons, and for the girls she had the black bonnets she'd finished before she and Joshua had married. She didn't mind all the work. She loved being a mother, enjoyed everything about the time she spent with them. And she relished the morning hours when she and Joshua were the only ones awake in a quiet house.

She had made Amish chicken pot pie earlier before inviting the girls to make dessert with her. The air was fragrant with cake and chicken, with vegetables and thin, flat noodles, making the house warm and cozy. Esther noted that the timer showed fifteen minutes left for the cupcakes. She made herself tea and sat down to enjoy it.

Commotion near the house's back entrance startled her until the door opened and Joshua stepped inside, bundled up against the cold in a woolen hat, navy blue coat and matching gloves. He stamped his feet on a mat near the door. Esther was surprised to see that snow covered him from head to toe. He managed to kick off his boots, but just barely.

"Joshua!" she cried, rising to help with his winter garments. Her husband was shivering too hard to accomplish the task. There was snow on his hat and jacket—and even his gloves. She tsk-tsked as she removed his hat and gloves. Then she worked to get his coat off before hanging it up. Esther eyed him with worry as he stood in stocking feet and a long-sleeve blue shirt with overalls, blowing on his hands to warm them.

"I slipped in the snow near the milking barn," he said, his lips quivering with the cold. "Didn't expect it to be that slick."

"Sit down, please," she urged him before she hurried to the stove to fix him a large mug of hot tea. He didn't say a word as he huddled in his chair, shaking as his body attempted to get warm. She placed the tea within his reach. "Here. This will help."

Joshua looked up at her. "*Danki.*"

Esther smiled as he cradled the mug, accepting the heat of it on his fingers. "You're *willkomm.* I had no idea it started to snow. I've been busy with the children and cooking and—"

He chuckled. "Relax, *frau.* You don't have to convince me that you've had your hands full. I know it's not easy taking care of four *kinner.*"

"I love them," she said.

His expression softened. "I know you do."

Magda entered the room with Leah following. "Are the cupcakes done—" Her eyes widened. "Dat! You're home!" She frowned as she looked from Esther to her father and back. "It's not lunchtime yet."

"With your *grossdaddi*'s and Nathaniel's help, we got

our morning chores done quickly, and it's a *gut* thing. It's snowing, windy and freezing cold!" Clearly feeling better, Joshua pretended to shudder to show his daughters how frigid it was outside.

"Do you have to go back?" Leah approached her father.

He took a sip of tea before answering. "Not until much later. I'm home for the afternoon."

Magda grinned. "That's *wunderbor!* Can we go sledding?"

"It's too cold right now with the wind," he told them. "But we will go soon. *Okey*?" He smiled as the girls eagerly bobbed their heads.

The windup timer went off, signaling that the cupcakes were done.

"We made cupcakes," Magda said with excitement. "Two kinds. One of them is your favorite."

Esther picked up two hot mitts and opened the oven door. The girls moved closer so that they could watch. "Careful," she warned gently, "or you'll get burned." She waited until after her daughters had taken a few steps back before she pulled out the two pans, one at a time, and set them on wire racks on the kitchen counter.

"They look *gut*!" Leah cried with delight. "Nice and full and...fluffy!"

Esther chuckled. "*Ja,* they do, don't they?" After the mini cakes cooled for a few minutes, she'd remove them from the pans and transfer them directly onto the racks.

"It smells *wunderbor* in here," Joshua said. "But I detect something else..."

"I made Amish chicken pot pie. I hope you like it." It occurred to her that she should have checked with him before deciding to make it.

"One of my favorite meals." He gazed at her with approval, which made her entire day. "Will it be ready for our midday meal?"

"Of course. I figured you would want something to warm you up inside." Esther stirred the pot, pleased with the way it looked.

"Where are the twins?" Joshua asked.

Magda pulled out a chair to sit by her father. "They're taking a nap."

"*Ja,* I've been keeping a close eye on them." Esther picked up her cup and took a sip. "I'll check on them again. They're bound to wake up soon."

Joshua finished his tea and stood. "We don't have to worry about them falling out of their cribs anymore—not since we converted them into toddler beds for them."

"*Ja,* well, I hope you're not upset with me," Esther said, afraid to tell him what she'd done, "but I—well, come and see for yourself."

He followed her to the twins' room, and she saw him examine the two-by-twelve piece of wood long enough to block off the doorway to keep the boys inside. "What's this?"

Esther shyly met his gaze. "I didn't want them to wake up and get hurt after racing out of the room. So, I made sure the room was safe for them and created a gate of sorts to keep them confined until I—we—could get them." She sighed. "I only wish the board was taller so they can't climb over it. Still, I'd thought it would slow them down."

"Est-er!" Jacob cried. He sat on the floor in the middle of the room with his brother playing with two wooden trucks between them. Both boys seemed content with their toys after getting out of bed.

Esther studied her husband as she tried to gauge his reaction to what she'd done. She had come up with the idea this morning after he'd left for work. She'd been running to the room every few minutes to make sure the twins were asleep and safe, fearful at what she'd discover if she didn't continually check on them. "Joshua?"

Her husband gazed at her for a long time, and she shifted uneasily under the intensity of his stare.

"Est-er!" Jacob climbed to his feet and approached the gate. His twin followed his lead. "Come out now?"

Esther smiled at the brothers. "*Ja,* you can come out." She reached over the gate and hefted Jacob into her arms. She handed the boy to his father and then lifted JJ, who beamed at her happily. "Magda, would you please remove the gate for me?"

Their eldest daughter obeyed while Esther carried JJ to the kitchen where she put him in his high chair. She was painfully aware that Joshua had yet to comment about the gate. Was he angry with her?

Joshua entered the room behind her and placed Jacob in his chair next to his brother's. He still hadn't said anything to her, and Esther blinked back tears. She had thought a gate was the best option for a pair of highly active two-year-old boys. Maybe she'd been wrong.

He had known her for not quite two months and had married her two weeks and a day ago, yet his wife continued to amaze him with her intelligence, her loving nature and her quick thinking. Every day she showed his children how much she loved them and saw to his comfort. She helped him get warm after being outside, fixed him meals, made him his favorite desserts and kept the house clean and the laundry done, all the while flashing her pretty smile.

Joshua suddenly realized that her lovely green eyes glistened, as if she fought tears, as she quietly handed out snacks to the children and poured each of them glasses of milk. "Esther."

She flinched before she looked at him. "*Ja?*"

"Please sit down beside me." He watched her with concern as she listened. "I need to tell you that you are brilliant and amazing. Using that wood as a gate was smart, and I'm happy you thought of it."

She blinked and her expression transformed before his eyes. His wife looked surprised by his words. "You are?" she whispered.

He leaned closer. "I am," he whispered in her ear.

Esther seemed stunned. "I thought that you were—"

"Upset with you?" he asked, suddenly understanding,

"*Ja.*" She no longer avoided his gaze. "I only want to keep everyone safe."

Joshua studied her with warmth. "And you have. I'm grateful that you agreed to be a part of our lives." He suddenly had more he wanted to say, but he knew he had to think about exactly what it was first. The idea of making theirs a real marriage had taken up residence in his thoughts…and his heart. What had seemed like the perfect solution for a man who was grieving for his late wife somehow now felt wrong…

She flashed him one of her bright smiles. "Would you like a chocolate cupcake? I haven't frosted them yet, but I know they are moist and delicious. I've made the recipe before."

"*Sighsogude.*" *Please.* "I would love one." He beamed as he watched her plate one for him. She was always conscious of his likes and dislikes, always eager to make a dessert she thought he might enjoy. And he did, every single time.

After snack time, the girls took their brothers into the living room, leaving him alone in the kitchen with Esther.

Joshua watched her stir the pot on the stove, and then whip up a bowl of frosting for the rest of the cupcakes.

He rose, went to the window and leaned his head against the glass as he gazed out into the wintry weather. Thoughts of Esther as more than just a wife of convenience had begun to intrude in his mind every moment of every day. He had never imagined he'd become so taken with her. He found he wasn't as consumed by his grief or guilt anymore either. How could he be when he had a sweet woman in his home…and in his life? He wasn't sure when it had happened. All he knew was he wanted more now. For himself and for her…together.

Sighing, he glanced down and saw that the hem of his overalls was still damp from the snow. Today, it was too icy and frigid outside—with the wind whipping through the air, making it colder—or he would have agreed to take the children sledding. Joshua went to don clean, dry triblend navy blue trousers before he entered his sons' room to get a closer look at Esther's childproof barrier. The makeshift gate was constructed of an oak board that had been stored in the barn after the renovations to the house. She must have gone outside to search for the wood right after he'd left for work, while the children were still sleeping. He knew exactly where she'd found it, near the barn door, in a place easily spotted as she'd entered the building.

Joshua decided to secure a second board on top of the one that Esther had brought in, to make the gate taller so the twins wouldn't be able to climb over it.

"Lunch!" Esther called, and Joshua realized with surprise that he'd been standing in the boys' doorway for some time.

When he entered the kitchen, the children were already seated. Esther stood at the stove, ladling the crustless chicken pot pie mixture into bowls for their daughters and sons. Joshua watched as she ladled larger portions for the two of them. He helped her carry the food to the table and waited with a smile when she sat down beside him.

He bowed his head. "Let us thank the Lord for our bounty."

The children became silent. Esther closed her eyes with her hands in her lap.

"Bless this family," Joshua said as he raised his head after offering up a prayer of his own. "Now let's eat!"

Lunch became a noisy affair with laughter and conversation. While snow fell outside and the wind blustered against the side of his house, he felt more than content in this kitchen, in this home with Esther and their children.

Chapter Sixteen

Joshua woke up with a start. He had fallen asleep with his head on the kitchen table. Tense, he stretched his shoulders to get the stiffness out and leaned back in his chair. He'd been awake for hours, his thoughts centered on Esther and their marriage before he'd finally dozed off. Why couldn't he relax? He had a plan and he had to stick with it. His feelings for his new wife were changing. She had opened his heart again.

On Christmas morning, he'd confess that he was falling in love with her. His wife deserved to be truly happy. He knew she thought of his children as hers by now, and he was grateful. But Esther deserved a child of her own—a brother or sister to his girls and twins. And he wanted it, too. A baby created by him and Esther. She was a natural mother, and he felt sure she'd be thrilled to bear a child, to add to their family. It wouldn't have to be right away, especially since the twins were currently a handful. When she was ready, he would be, too.

Joshua gazed into the dark as he wondered how best to propose a change in their relationship. He wasn't sure when his feelings toward her had grown. He only knew they had, and he suspected hers had too. He closed his eyes and calmed himself. He had just over a week to figure out what to say.

The silence in the room seemed too complete. He missed having her near, the way she smiled as she made breakfast. The grin when one of the children said something that tickled her.

Sensing a presence, Joshua frowned and stood. He made his way to the living room and immediately saw her. Eyes closed, Esther sat with her head at an angle, her body slumped against the chairback. A battery-powered lantern rested on the table, its light turned low. Concerned, he hurried to her and lowered himself to his knees. The last thing he wanted was to frighten her.

"Esther," he whispered. "*Frau.*"

She sighed heavily as she stretched and opened her eyes. Esther jolted when she caught sight of him crouched at her feet. "Joshua," she gasped.

"It's the middle of the night." He studied her with concern. "Why are you out of bed?"

"I couldn't sleep." She quickly shoved whatever she had on her lap into a fabric bag on the floor beside her.

Joshua rose to his feet, pulled a chair close to her and sat down, facing her. He gently took her hand and began to stroke the back of it with his fingers. "Why can't you sleep?"

With her other hand, she pulled her single braid from her back to her front across one shoulder. "I'm sorry if I disturbed you. You shouldn't be up because of me. You need to work early tomorrow."

He studied the tote at her feet before meeting her gaze. "Trying to tire yourself with mending?"

Esther shook her head. "Christmas is only eight days away. I have gifts to finish, and I can't work on them during the day when the children will see."

He felt warm and soft inside at her confession. "Esther, you can't continue to work at night and be tired the next day."

"I didn't plan to be up this long," she assured him. "I'll take *gut* care of our children. I won't let anything bad happen to them."

"I never doubted it." Joshua hated to see the worry in her green eyes, as if she was afraid of doing something wrong and losing her place in his children's life, in his life. "My *vadder* has been asking when he and Alta can see their grandchildren. Why don't we let them take the *kinner* for the day. That will help, *ja*?"

She blinked in the lantern light. "You'd do that for me?"

Enjoying the smooth skin of her hand under his touch, he searched her face. "You are my wife. Of course I'd do that for you. I'll give you anything you need."

He watched as she fought tears. "*Danki*, Joshua."

Retaining hold of her hand, Joshua stood. "You should get some sleep." He smiled when she allowed him to pull her up.

"Are you coming?"

He shook his head. "Not yet. I've been up for a while, too. Best to take the opportunity to rest before the children wake up in about—" he glanced at the living-room wall clock "—six hours."

"Joshua—"

"Go, Esther. I'll be fine."

He watched her leave the room and smiled. Making gifts in the middle of the night. She worked too hard. There must be something he could do to make her life easier. She deserved only the best.

Esther had slept hard. She didn't find it difficult to get up when the time came to make her husband's breakfast, as she felt quite rested. She was surprised to find him making coffee when she entered the kitchen. After enjoying eggs, bacon and toast—he was easy to cook for—Joshua bundled up against the cold.

"I'll talk with my *dat* today," he said, and she could only nod with a smile before he left the house. She watched him drive the buggy off the property with a yearning for something more with him.

The girls woke up two hours later. "Can we have pancakes?" Leah asked as she and Magda entered the kitchen, already dressed.

"I'll be happy to make them for you." Esther pulled out a mixing bowl and the ingredients for pancakes from a recipe she'd learned from her mother. "Are your *bruders* up yet?"

"They weren't when we checked a few minutes ago." Magda approached where Esther stood at the counter. "I can set the table."

"That would be *gut*." Esther cracked two eggs into the bowl and whipped them with a fork. "Leah, would you please check on the twins again for me?" She knew that if they were up, the boys would be safe in their rooms, thanks to Joshua, who had added another board to the top of the gate she'd made. But she'd been working to potty train them, and the sooner she got them into the bathroom once they were up the better. Jacob seemed to be catching on fine. JJ wasn't as eager to follow his brother's lead.

She had finished making the pancake batter when Leah called out from the back of the house. "The boys are up!"

After setting down her spoon, Esther hurried to the twins' room. Sure enough, they lay on their beds with open eyes.

As soon as she got them ready for the day, she brought

them into the kitchen and put them in their high chairs. "We're having pancakes for breakfast," she told them.

"Pancakes! Pancakes!" the twins exclaimed at the same time.

"Magda, nice job on the table," Esther praised and her daughter grinned.

It wasn't long before each child was at the table eating pancakes with butter and maple syrup. Having eaten with Joshua earlier, Esther wasn't hungry. She made herself coffee and then took a seat and watched the children enjoy their meal.

Someone rapped on the metal back door twice, and Esther peered out the window. Recognizing the couple outside, she smiled as she let them in. "Jonas, Alta," she greeted her in-laws. "It's *wunderbor* to see you."

Brown eyes so like Joshua's grew warm as Jonas gazed at her. "We'd hoped you'd allow us to take your children for the day."

Alta nodded. "It seems like forever since we spent time with them."

"Children, would you like to go with your *grosseldre* for a visit?" Esther studied their expressions.

"I thought we'd make Christmas cookies," Alta told them. "It may seem early, but I decided we can practice decorating them."

"Can we eat them?" Leah asked as she picked up her plate and utensils then carried them to the sink.

"*Ja,* what fun is making them if we don't get to eat them?" Jonas said.

"I'm in," Magda said with delight.

Leah looked excited. "Me, too."

"We go, too!" Jacob exclaimed.

JJ bobbed his head. "Me go, too!"

With Alta's help, the children were soon bundled against the cold. As they followed their *grossmammi* out of the house, Esther turned to Jonas. "I appreciate this."

"It's our pleasure," her father-in-law said. "Joshua explained the situation, but we love having them. And it has been too long."

"I can fetch them this afternoon," Esther assured him.

"We'll bring them back after supper. I think Alta already has plans for them." Then Jonas left, and Esther watched as he climbed into the driver's side of his buggy.

In the back seat, Magda waved vigorously at Esther through the window, a huge grin on her face before the buggy left the property.

With the children gone, Esther suffered a sense of loss. It felt lonely in the house without their noisy presence to keep her company. But Joshua had been right. She couldn't continue to work on Christmas presents in the middle of the night. She needed her sleep to keep up with the twins and their sisters.

After a quick kitchen cleanup, Esther retrieved her cloth bag from the floor where she'd hid it behind her chair. Inside it, she kept navy blue yarn and her crochet hook…and the gifts she'd made for the twins. Then she set up to work in the living room.

While her husband was absent, she thought it best to finish his Christmas gift first—a thick navy blue scarf that was two-thirds of the way done. With the current bitter cold and the prospect of it continuing throughout the winter, she'd decided that a comfortable scarf would keep Joshua warm whenever he was outdoors.

Before she started crocheting, she went to the kitchen to prepare a meal for Joshua's lunch. The snow had melted during the last two days, but it was still frigid outside. Her husband would need something hot and hearty to warm him when he came home.

She decided pot roast would be delicious and easy enough to fix. It would take close to three hours to cook, but it was still early enough for her to prepare the browned top round, seasonings, onions, carrots and potatoes with slices of crispy bacon for added flavor. She found joy in fixing a meal for her family. Esther loved running the household and caring for the children.

Once she put everything in a stainless steel Dutch oven, she set it on the stove to simmer. Then she placed bread dough in the oven. There was nothing like fresh bread slathered in butter to eat with a meal.

Satisfied that the food would be ready in time, Esther returned to her crocheting in the living room. While she worked on the scarf for her husband, she thought about her changing feelings toward him. She never meant to allow him into her heart. But how could she not care for the kind, attentive and thoughtful man Joshua was? Loving his children was one thing, but feeling the same way for their father promised only heartbreak for her.

Besides finishing Joshua's gift, she needed to figure out something special to give to her parents and in-laws. She was grateful for this time to get things done and to plan.

After an hour, Esther studied the finished scarf for her husband and smiled. She hoped Joshua would like it. She'd made similar ones for his sons. They'd go well with the black bonnets she'd made for the girls, which would provide extra warmth when worn over their organza prayer *kapps*.

A quick glance at the clock two hours later had her scurrying to put away the Christmas gifts and hide the gift satchel from prying eyes, including her husband's gorgeous brown ones. Once everything was out of sight, Esther set the table for her and Joshua and then put on a pot of coffee as she waited for him.

After he looked in on the cows and heifers in the heifer barn to make sure they had water and feed, Joshua checked in with his father and then headed home. He was glad the snow was gone. Driving could be dangerous on snowy and icy roads. If the precipitation held off, they'd have an easy holiday traveling on Second Christmas to visit family and friends. On December 25, or what everyone within the community regarded as First Christmas, he, Esther and the children would have a quiet day together. Joshua anticipated the day with excitement because he was eager to talk with Esther about changing the conditions of their marriage. He wanted her in his life as a true wife.

It wasn't long before he made the turn onto the road where he and his family lived. As he drove closer to the house, he began to doubt he should wait until Christmas to have the conversation with Esther. His wife was home alone. Their children weren't expected back until after supper. Dat had said that there was no need for him to return to work, which meant that he and Esther would spend the rest of the day together.

Joshua flipped on his blinker and pulled into his driveway. He would talk with her today. And if all went well, they would have not only a future together but a child, too. He parked near the barn, opened the door and steered the buggy inside. Then he unhitched his gelding and moved him into a stall, closing the barn door shut behind him before he headed toward the house.

Joshua couldn't keep from grinning as, with hope in his heart, he opened the back door and entered the kitchen.

He was eager to see the woman who had done the unexpected. Esther had eased his grief and filled the hole that had opened inside him after Anna's death. "*Hallo*, wife. I'm home!"

Esther came from a back room, her lips curving when she saw him. "Joshua. I hope you're hungry."

"I am. And it smells *wunderbor* in here." He tugged off his hat and gloves then pushed them into the sleeve of his navy blue coat before he hung up the garment.

"Pot roast with vegetables and fresh bread." She opened the oven door and pulled out a foil-wrapped loaf from the middle rack. "Please sit. Would you like a cup of coffee? I have root beer, too."

"Coffee, please. The snow is gone, but it's still freezing out." Joshua pulled out a chair and took a seat. "I saw the children before I left. The twins were napping, but the girls were having a *gut* time decorating cookies."

"*Ja*. Alta told them making and decorating cookies would be good practice for the ones made closer to Christmas." Esther transferred the meat and vegetables into a serving bowl and brought it to the table. She went back for the bread and unwrapped it before she placed it on a cutting board with a knife. "Alta had to reassure Leah that they could eat some of the cookies."

Joshua chuckled. "I bet she did." He watched her spoon food onto a plate for him and added two pieces of sliced bread. Suddenly noting the shadows under her eyes, he had the strongest urge to tell her to relax. She clearly hadn't slept well last night, which concerned him. "You didn't have to do all this work."

She frowned. "It's no trouble." Esther chewed on her lower lip as she handed him his plate. "You don't want pot roast? I… I should have asked you."

"*Nay,* Esther. You don't have to ask me what to cook." He softened his expression as he leaned back in his chair and studied her. "You barely slept last night, and I was worried about you." He smiled. "I love pot roast." Joshua tasted the meat and vegetables, which were delicious. The roast was perfectly seasoned and the vegetables were the right consistency. "You are an excellent cook. This is tasty."

Esther sat, staring at him for a long moment before she took her first bite of the meal. She beamed at him, clearly happy how the dish had turned out.

"Did you get done what you needed?" Joshua began to eat in earnest, his eyes on her pretty face as he tried to read her thoughts from her expression.

"I did." She paused to chew a bite of buttered bread, then swallowed. "The only thing left is to decide what to give our families."

"We still have time." He thought for a moment. "What about some Christmas treats like fudge or butter brickle?"

"Or poinsettias," she suggested.

"Both will work, don't you think?" Joshua said, eliciting a smile from her. There was a closeness between them that made him feel good inside. He knew there wouldn't be a better time than now to talk about their future. "There is something I'd like to discuss with you." Because he was nervous, his tone was sharper than he'd intended.

She frowned. "What's wrong?"

"There is nothing wrong," he assured her quickly when she suddenly looked uneasy. "I've been thinking about us...about our marriage." Joshua had to pause a minute to breathe, to seek his inner calm. "First, I must apologize. I feel as if I've taken advantage of you, and that's not fair."

"I don't understand." Esther seemed to relax. "I knew

what our life would be like when I agreed to marry you. You don't have to apologize about anything."

Softening his expression, he shook his head. "*Ja,* I do. I shouldn't have put conditions on our life together." He reached for her hand, cradling it lovingly between his larger ones. "And I wanted—needed—to tell you that I think we should consider removing those conditions. I'd like for us to have a child together. It's not fair for you to sacrifice everything for me and the needs of the children."

To his surprise, she turned pale. "So, what you're saying is—"

"I want a real marriage with you, Esther. To have a child of our own. We can certainly manage five children as well as we do the four we have now."

Esther shoved back her chair. "You want me to have a *bubbel*. With you."

He smiled. "*Ja.*"

Avoiding his gaze, she stood. "I'm sorry, Joshua, but I can't," she whispered, her eyes filling with tears. "What you want…it's just not possible."

He was momentarily stunned as Esther reached for her cloak. Then she ran out into the cold, leaving him sitting there before he had a chance to react.

What happened? Joshua had felt sure they'd been developing feelings for each other. At least, he had. But Esther? "I guess I was wrong," he murmured with a sudden pain in his chest.

A gust of wind struck the house just then, slamming against the siding, rattling window glass. Worried, Joshua looked out the window. The sky had darkened. The wind picked up, tossing unsecured items around the yard. A clay flowerpot. A plastic Adirondack chair that had been stored behind the house.

Joshua's concern became alarm when he didn't see his wife anywhere. He donned his coat and hat then went out into the blustering cold to look for her.

She wouldn't go far, would she? Joshua didn't know. He'd never expected her startling reaction to what he'd hoped would bring them closer as man and wife. To bring them joy.

Please, Lord, help me find her quickly. Please keep Esther safe.

Chapter Seventeen

Shivering uncontrollably, Esther huddled behind the barn to shelter from the wind. She had her cloak but no scarf or gloves, and her *kapp* did nothing to provide warmth.

He wants me to have a child, but I can't!

Under other circumstances, she'd be overjoyed that Joshua wished to change things between them. But she couldn't give him what he wanted. She'd always known how important it was to a man for a woman to give birth. Which was why, since her diagnosis, she'd never spent time with potential beaux or attended youth singings. The last thing she needed was to have to confess her inability to have a baby to anyone, especially someone who could potentially become serious with her. So Joshua's offer of a marriage of convenience had seemed like an answer to her prayers.

She shook from the cold as she hugged herself, tucking her hands under her armpits beneath her winter woolen cloak to heat them. The wind made the frigid air feel worse. Esther knew she was a fool for hiding behind the outbuilding in the harsh weather. The interior of the barn would be warmer, but she needed time alone, and she knew Joshua would search for her there first. And there was nowhere else to go. Her parents didn't know about her medical condition, and she wasn't going to admit it now.

Would her husband cast her aside if he knew the truth? It was possible he wouldn't. After all, they had gone into the marriage knowing what was expected—a marriage of convenience. Esther knew she'd upheld her part of the agreement. They had gotten along well and become friends. But what if his desire to have another baby changed things between them that made it too difficult to go on as man and wife?

Shivering, Esther pulled her cloak over her knees to hold in her body heat. She knew she couldn't stay outside long or she might suffer frostbite. And she didn't want to get sick. Avoiding him wouldn't help matters. And the fact that he hadn't come after her told her everything she needed to know.

Her abdomen cramped, a sign that she was stressed or that it would soon be time for her monthly cycle. She suspected the latter. *Nay*, not now! *Please, Lord, give me guidance and the strength to face the uncertain future ahead.*

"Esther! *Esther!*" Joshua's voice faded with a wind gust until the air calmed for a moment. "Where are you, *frau*? Please tell me you're *oll recht*!"

Pressing her hands against her lower belly, she struggled to her feet. "I'm here!" she called back. Her hands felt frozen, her nose cold. There wasn't any part of her that didn't feel the bite of the weather.

"Esther!" Joshua sounded closer. "Call out to me. Please tell me where you are!"

There was no denying her husband's concern. "Behind the barn!" she managed to cry out. He had come for her. She'd heard the alarm in his voice. Esther started to sob. She loved her life with Joshua and the children. She loved *him* and didn't want to lose him.

Then suddenly he was there, his brown eyes filled with

worry. "*Liebchen*," he gasped, reaching to pull her close to warm and comfort her. "Come inside. Everything will be *oll recht*."

"I'm sorry. So sorry." She couldn't control her tears.

"Please. You'll catch your death." He caught her hand and she relished the heat of his grasp through his glove. "Let's go back to the *haus*. We can talk. Whatever is wrong, we'll work through it."

Esther allowed him to lead her back to the house. Once inside, he helped her remove her cloak. Then she watched Joshua put the kettle on and pull out two tea bags from a tin on the counter.

"The oven is hot. You should feel better soon." He took down two mugs and left them close to the stove. "I'll be *recht* back. I'm going to stoke the fire in the woodstove." Then he left the kitchen, leaving her to worry about their cold meal.

She sensed his return while she was putting the food into the oven. She stumbled as she stepped back, but he caught her before she fell. She met his gaze. "*Danki*."

He frowned when she gasped and clutched her stomach. "You need your pain reliever," he said with concern. "Do you have anything stronger than acetaminophen?"

"There," she said, pointing toward a top kitchen cabinet. "Ibuprofen. On the second shelf."

He took it down and then gestured toward her chair. "Sit. I'll take care of you." He tipped out two capsules and then filled a glass with water at the sink.

"I have to—" She bolted to the bathroom, slamming the door behind her.

"Esther, are you *oll recht*?" Joshua had followed her.

"I'll be out in a minute," she called. She did what she had to do and then opened the door to find him waiting for her.

"*Frau*—" he began.

"I'm fine." She felt lightheaded as she reentered the kitchen.

Joshua brought her pain reliever to the table. Still standing, she quickly swallowed the pills with water.

"I should eat a couple of crackers or something with these," she told him.

He hurried to find her something to protect her stomach. He cut a slice of the bread she'd made, then brought it to the table. "Will this work? Do you want butter?"

"This is fine and *nay* to butter." She got down a few bites of the bread.

He watched her carefully as if afraid she would break, but he didn't say a word.

"Joshua." Esther stood, using her hand on the table surface to steady herself. She felt guilty. It didn't seem right for him to do anything for her after she'd run from the house, from him.

"I told you to sit, *frau,*" he replied sternly.

She blinked, shocked by his tone, and obeyed but couldn't stop the fresh onslaught of tears. Clutching her stomach, she bent over. Esther tried to control her emotions, but the pain ripped away her attempt at restraint.

The kettle whistled and Joshua prepared two cups of hot tea. Facing her, he stilled a moment when he saw her before he brought them to the table. She kept her head down, but she could feel his stare. With a tsk-tsking sound that made her look up, Joshua abruptly left the room. When he returned, he wrapped a quilt snuggly around her shoulders. "*Danki,*" she whispered.

Without a word, he filled up a hot-water bottle and opened the edges of the blanket and settled it on her abdomen. She shifted uncomfortably at first, and then the heat from it began to settle in. It felt good.

Joshua watched as she took her first sip of hot tea. He was relieved that Esther was all right, but he also felt angry that she'd run out in the frigid weather to avoid talking to him. Why had she run away? Because she hated the idea of becoming intimate with him? Why was she unable to trust that he'd listen to her concerns?

He kept silent as he eyed her. She cradled the cup, the heat from the porcelain seeming to thaw her hands. Her red skin was returning to normal, her fingers no longer curled and shaky. She didn't speak and refused to meet his gaze. Her eyes remained focused on her hot beverage. It was as if he wasn't in the room. Joshua shook his head, his jaw clenching, as the tension between them spiked.

It was time to discuss why she'd felt that her only choice was to flee.

"Talk to me, Esther." He pulled his chair closer to hers and maneuvered it so that he would face her when he sat down. With a scowl, he took a seat. "You said you can't. Can't what? Become my wife in the traditional sense?" Joshua watched as she closed off her expression.

He could see she was struggling not to cry. He hated seeing her this way, but he couldn't help how disappointed he felt. Joshua was still upset that she'd dashed outside. He needed to ensure she wouldn't run from him again at the slightest provocation. Still, her tears got to him. Feeling terrible that he'd been harsh with her, he softened his tone. "Esther, talk to me. Whatever it is, we'll figure it out." He leaned forward, closing the gap between them.

"It's hard for me to explain. I can't—" She swallowed hard. "I can't have a baby."

"You're not ready," he said with sudden understanding.

"*Nay*." She shook her head. "I can't give you a child. Ever."

Joshua frowned. "What are you saying? That you don't want my child?"

She inhaled sharply. "I'm barren. I am physically unable to conceive or carry a child to term."

"You're—" He gazed at her with shock. Never in his wildest thoughts had he believed the reason for her tears was *this*.

Esther hung her head. "I'm sorry."

"There is nothing to apologize for." Thinking hard how best to respond, he tugged on his beard. "You're certain?" He purposely kept his voice soft.

Nodding, she shifted on her seat then reached beneath the blanket to do something with the water bottle. When she didn't pull it out, he figured she had adjusted the heat to a better area that would help her most effectively.

She hesitated. "I have a condition called endometriosis," she said. "There are growths inside me that cause cramps and that the doctor said would prevent me from conceiving."

Joshua reached for her hands and held them gently within his grasp. "I know you suffer pain, but how bad does it get and how often?"

Esther shrugged. "Sometimes the pain is mild, while at other times it's much worse. I'm thankful that over-the-counter pain relievers usually help to control it." She held his gaze with glistening green eyes. "I've always wanted to give birth, but I can't." She blinked rapidly and he saw the sheen of fresh tears.

"Do you think I would reject you because of this?" he asked. "I'm sorry. It's *oll recht*. I wish I'd known. I would never intentionally hurt you. I'm happy with my brood of four. You are a *wunderbor frau*...and—" he paused to search for the right words "—I care about you." Releasing her hands, he sat back. "You shouldn't have run from me. You need to tell me whenever you're upset. I won't judge you, Esther. We are together for life."

"*Danki.*" A small smile transformed her features, and he was unable to look away. "I..." She bit her lip as if afraid to continue.

Joshua decided he would postpone further discussion about changing their marriage to something real between them. It didn't seem like the right time. She was already on the verge of tears and he didn't want to press her. But he refused to wait too long to talk more. "Shall we finish our meal?"

"The food!" With a cry of dismay, Esther sprang from her seat.

"*Nay.* Sit," he ordered, more sharply than he'd intended. She'd winced as she got up. "Let me get it." He used hot mitts to retrieve their plates from the oven. "Frau, what did I say?" he said, softening his tone. She still stood, with tears shimmering in her green eyes. "I'll take care of you. Please sit, *liebchen.*"

Blinking rapidly, she obeyed. As he placed her meal before her, Joshua hid a smile. Esther looked extremely uncomfortable having him serve her. His new wife would have to get used to his help, especially during the times she was hurting.

He refilled her teacup before he joined her at the table. Then they ate in silence. He had told her the truth—that it didn't matter to him that she couldn't conceive a child. It would have been wonderful if she could, but that she was unable to didn't lessen his regard for her. As he continued to eat without a word, he replayed their conversation in his head. Clearly, she'd been distraught over telling him that she was barren. Yet, she'd confessed her desire to have a baby. But was there more? Was she afraid at the thought of being intimate with him?

Joshua sighed. He'd admitted he cared about her. Should he have told her his feelings for her had started to change? To grow? Perhaps in time. He had to be sure that he wasn't caught up in the intensity of the moment before he said anything. He'd loved Anna. It bothered him that he'd forgotten that. And he became overwhelmed with guilt all of a sudden.

Pushing his remorse aside, Joshua set down his fork and leaned back in his chair, purposely drawing his wife's attention. "I don't want you to worry." He reached for her hand and gave it a gentle reassuring squeeze before letting go. "We don't have to change our relationship."

She nodded. He should have been relieved, but her quick agreement bothered him.

"Are you feeling better?" he asked, studying her closely.

He saw her swallow. "I will be soon."

She looked too pale, and he couldn't help his concern. "Maybe you should lie down."

Esther shook her head. "I'd like to eat with you. I'll be fine."

"After we eat, then," he said, with a hint of command in his tone. He refused to see her suffer when it would be better for her to rest. "I'll clean up."

"Joshua," she started to object.

"I'll clean up," he repeated firmly and was satisfied when she silently agreed.

After their meal, he stood. "Rest," he said.

She didn't argue, which told him she needed a nap to feel better. Joshua wondered what he could do to help her as he watched her leave the room. And then he went to work, clearing the table and washing dishes. When he was done, he checked on her and was glad to find her fast asleep on the living-room sofa. He hoped she'd feel better after sleeping. If not, he'd urge her into bed and then deal with the children when they came home. He was used to being alone with them.

Joshua sighed. He'd told Esther that they didn't have to change their relationship, but in truth, he wanted more in their marriage, so all he could do right now was to pray and be patient. Esther's warm smile for him, her easy companionship and her love for his children had deepened his feelings for her. He'd do whatever was necessary to prove that he was worthy of being a true husband to her. And he would wait for her to care for him in the same way, so that she'd want their marriage to be a real one. Joshua asked *Gott* to help him and promised Him that he'd do his best to make his lovely wife happy for the rest of their lives together.

Chapter Eighteen

Joshua watched his children get out of his father's buggy an hour later. He figured Esther was still asleep and he hadn't wanted to wake her because she needed rest. But then she entered the kitchen, looking much better, if still a little pale.

Their little ones burst into the house, accompanied by their grandfather. Joshua could tell that Esther was as happy as he to see them.

"Did you miss us?" Magda said.

"We did." Esther smiled. "How were the cookies?"

"*Wunderbor!*" Leah hopped up and down with excitement. "Grossmammi Alta baked them but we got to decorate them with icing and sprinkles!"

"Did you bring us any?" Joshua asked after a quick glance at his father.

With a chuckle, Magda held out a brown paper bag. "You should try them now before we eat them!" She laughed, and to his delight, Esther joined in.

"*Danki*, Jonas, for having them," she said sincerely.

"It was our pleasure." His father studied his grandchildren. "Be *gut* and help Esther and your *vadder*," he said.

"We will!" Leah assured him.

The girls waved through the window as his *dat* left.

When their grandparents had come for the children early

that morning, the twins had been reasonably calm for two-year-old boys. Now, they were more than a handful after apparently eating too many of Alta's sweets. But still, Esther showered them with patience and love, despite the change in their behavior since their return. And it was clear that his sons loved her, too. She found a way to keep them busy and quiet until it was time for bed, and she checked on them often to make sure they had enough to do.

Joshua couldn't help but be amazed by her. She'd been suffering earlier, but he was the only one who knew. If she still had pain, she hid it well. But then he looked closely and saw shadows beneath her eyes, which should have been absent after napping.

Esther never lost patience with their children. Sometimes his wife disappeared for a few moments of needed privacy. And then she'd return as if nothing bothered her. She smiled often and showered the children with attention. Every time he locked gazes with her, Joshua felt grateful for her presence.

By the time their *kinner* were asleep in their beds, he recognized that Esther was exhausted and hurting. He followed her into the living room after grabbing a pain reliever and hot-water bottle. Her eyes widened when she saw what he'd brought her. "Joshua," she breathed. "You knew just what I needed." She straightened in her chair, pulling up the quilt covering her to keep her warm.

"I can tell when you're not feeling well." He handed her the pills with water then watched with satisfaction as she took her medicine. Then he gave her the hot-water bottle, and she took it and placed it on her abdomen beneath the quilt.

"*Danki,* Joshua," she murmured.

"You're *willkomm*, Esther." Joshua went into the kitchen

for a snack and then decided to make her sweetened hot milk to help her relax.

Her eyes widened when a while later he checked in on her and gave her a mug of the milk. He sat in the chair next to her and kept a watchful eye on her.

His wife took a sip and smiled at him. "This is *wunderbor*, Joshua. I love hot milk, and you sweetened it perfectly."

Esther seemed to be feeling better, but he couldn't help worrying. Joshua didn't understand why she had to continue to suffer. He hated seeing her in pain. Surely, something could be done to help her. Perhaps he'd see a doctor and discuss her condition, so that he'd have a better understanding of it.

She finished her hot milk and set the mug on the small table he'd moved closer to her earlier. "I'm feeling much better," she murmured sleepily. "*Danki.*"

Studying his beautiful, thoughtful wife, he offered a prayer of thanks to the Lord for bringing her into his life.

Esther, with Magda's assistance, decorated the house for Christmas during the days that followed. Joshua had cut and brought home pine boughs and holly, which she used to bring holiday cheer to every room of the house. When his wife asked Leah to join her and Magda, Leah giggled and quickly pitched in to help.

Joshua enjoyed spending time with her each night, sitting side by side in chairs with their feet up on their ottomans or on the sofa, content to have her close. But he wanted more. Would she ever be ready for their marriage to become real? He couldn't ask her again; he didn't want to scare her away. And he was surprised to realize how desperately he wanted the change.

Sometime during the last week, Joshua had decided

he wouldn't talk with a doctor on his own. He thought it would be better if Esther checked in to see if a physician could offer a better solution to her health issues. He could accompany her and learn more then. While Joshua hated seeing her in pain, he wouldn't talk with her about making a doctor's appointment until after the holidays. So far this week she'd been fine, with no sign of the cramps that could cause her to feel ill.

It was important to him that they enjoy their first Christmas together as a family. Would Esther like his gifts for her birthday as well as Christmas? Later, in January, he'd make it a priority to focus on her health and well-being. Joshua continued to pray daily that he'd be able to convince her to seek professional help, even if she didn't believe it necessary. However, he could be as determined and stubborn as she.

Esther was excited. She had finished her handcrafted Christmas gifts for Joshua and the children, and she'd used the money she'd saved from when she cleaned houses to buy a board game called Aggravation for the family, and a new pair of gloves and a box of chocolates for her husband, all from Kings General Store.

It was finally Christmas Eve and she'd prepared a special meal of cinnamon apple–pork chops with dried corn casserole and mashed potatoes. Esther made homemade yeast rolls to accompany the meal and placed them in a cloth-lined breadbasket.

"Dinner!" she called out as she put the basket on the table by the other food.

The children rushed into the room, followed closely by her handsome husband. She watched with a grin as everyone eagerly took their seats, even the twins who now sat in booster seats on kitchen chairs. Esther had suggested the change for their sons to see how things went. If it didn't go well, they could go back to putting the boys in their high chairs.

Joshua said grace, and Esther served the children and her husband before taking some for herself.

"Tomorrow is Christmas," she said.

"Are we going to see Grossdaddi Jonas and Grossmammi Alta?" Magda asked.

"*Ja,* but not tomorrow," Joshua said. "Christmas is just for the six of us. We'll visit your *grosseldre* on Second Christmas, the next day."

Esther nodded. "Second Christmas is the day for visiting. We'll see both sets of *grosseldre* and stop in to see *endie* Fannie, *onkel* David and your cousin Rose, too."

"I can't wait until Second Christmas!" Leah exclaimed.

"It will be a *wunderbor* day here tomorrow, too." Joshua caught Esther's gaze, and she felt her cheeks heat.

"I'll make something special to eat for us," she told the children. "We can make cookies this afternoon, and I'll let you decorate them."

Their daughters appeared eager at the prospect. "May we eat them?" Magda asked.

She smiled. "You can have a couple each, but I thought we'd bring some to share with family members on Second Christmas."

After learning that the next two days were both holidays, the children's excitement kept them awake longer than usual that night. Esther didn't mind. She brought out puzzles and wooden toys for them to play with in the living room while she sat beside her husband on the sofa. Being this close to Joshua made her long to be a true wife to him.

"*Gut* idea using puzzles for them to wind down," Joshua murmured in her ear, his breath warm against her skin.

"They love puzzles." Esther felt blessed to have such a kind and wonderful man in her life. He had given her a family of her own, and she loved him more than she'd ever expected.

A sudden twinge in her lower abdomen made her wince. Wondering why it was happening again so soon, she breathed through the pain. The last thing she wanted was to worry him.

Joshua reached over her lap to cover her hands with his own. "You're hurting. Again."

"I'll be fine," she assured him, managing a smile. *Please, Lord, not now, not for the Christmas holidays. Please make it go away quickly.*

"Esther," he scolded, clearly unconvinced. Joshua stood. "*Oll recht*, children. It's time for bed."

"*Okey.*" Magda put the puzzle pieces in its box. She stood and held out her hand for Leah.

She and Joshua tucked the children in bed and wished them goodnight.

After the little ones had settled in, Esther went into the kitchen to make sure everything was ready for Christmas Day. She had planned to make fried sugar doughnuts in the morning as a special breakfast treat, and now debated whether she should make them tonight instead.

"Esther, come sit with me and rest for a while," Joshua said when he found her. He captured her hand and gently tugged her back into the living room. He sat on the sofa and pulled her to sit beside him. "You did too much today."

She frowned. "Not any more than usual."

"So what you're saying is that you were this busy before

you married me." To her surprise, he tucked her against his side with his arm around her shoulders.

"I..." Esther knew that she was busier as a wife and mother, but she didn't mind. She loved every second of her new life. She was just tired of dealing with the cramps that continued to plague her.

Being this close to Joshua made her feel flustered. She'd never expected he might like sitting together as much as she did. Or maybe he simply wanted her to enjoy the moment.

"Well?" His deep voice rumbled against her, making her overly aware of his proximity.

If anyone else saw them, Esther thought, they would believe them a happily married couple in love. The fact that they weren't made her sad.

"I may be busier now, but this is what I want, Joshua. I like my life here." She sighed and looked up at him. "With you and our *kinner*."

His brown eyes were warm and affectionate as he held her gaze. "I know you do, but the fact remains that you need to rest while you have the chance." He smirked. "And spend as much alone time as you can with your husband."

She widened her eyes. It seemed as if his feelings for her had changed. She prayed it was true. "*Okey*."

"*Okey*?" He arched an eyebrow.

Her lips twitched as she stared at him. "*Ja*. Why?"

"I'm surprised you're willing." Joshua continued to study her. "Since you're being so agreeable, I want to bring up something that you might not like, but I want you to listen and then we won't talk about it again. At least, not until after the holidays. *Oll recht*?"

"You're scaring me." She started to withdraw but he held onto her steadily.

"Nothing to fear," he assured her. "I was going to wait but…"

She was shocked when she felt tension in his shoulders as he stiffened. "What is it?"

"I'd like you to think about seeing a doctor about your cramps…your endo—"

"Endometriosis," she said. Esther closed her eyes, afraid to do what he suggested. But she was tired of hurting, especially when she had children to care for. Maybe there was something other than surgery that would help with her pain.

"Esther…" he said huskily. "I'm worried about you."

"I know," she said after a brief hesitation.

"What do you think, *liebchen*?" He brushed her cheek with the back of his fingers. "Will you consider it?"

His touch felt good against her skin. "I'll think about it," she breathed.

Apparently, she'd given him the right response because he pulled her tightly against him.

"*Gut*," he murmured. "There is one more thing we need to discuss."

"*Ja?*"

"Esther, I know you agreed to a marriage in name only, and I thought that's what I wanted. But something inside me has shifted. I never thought I'd feel alive again, but you…" He swallowed hard. "It's impossible not to be affected by you. Your warm, kind heart and amazing capacity to give of yourself to our *kinner*—to me—have made a huge difference. And that's only two of the many reasons why you've healed my heart." She held her breath as he paused. "Esther Miller, *mein* wife, I've begun to develop feelings for you. I hope that someday you'll feel the same way about me."

"Joshua," she whispered. "What are you saying?"

His brown eyes softened with affection and something

more. Something that gave her hope. "That I love you and pray that someday you'll love me too."

Tears spilled from her eyes as she cupped her hand over her mouth.

"It doesn't matter if you can't have a child," he quickly assured her. "It's you that matters to me, just the way you are." He appeared uncertain when she didn't speak. "We don't have to change anything," he murmured, entwining their fingers.

Shaking her head, Esther pulled her hand from her mouth and covered their joined fingers. "*Nay*, we do," she whispered as a tear escaped a green eye to slide down her cheek. "This changes everything. We can't go back to what we had, Joshua, because you see… I have fallen for you, too."

He stared at her as if wondering if he'd heard her correctly. "Did you just say—"

Esther laughed. "I did, *mein* husband. I love you more than I ever expected to love any man. You are everything I'd ever hoped and prayed for."

It was his turn to fight tears. "Praise *Gott*," he said, his voice filled with emotion.

Then he bent his head and kissed her. It was at that moment that Esther knew she would do anything he asked of her, including seeing a doctor. The last thing she wanted was to cause him worry.

"I'll make a doctor's appointment." His kiss had made her swoon. "I might not be able to see the same doctor. It's been years and I wouldn't be surprised if she's moved on."

"*Danki*," he said huskily. "Our *kinner* will be up early." Joshua stood. "We should get some rest." He held out his hand, and she accepted it.

Tomorrow was not only Christmas, but it was also her birthday, although she doubted that her husband would remember. Which was fine. He'd already given so much. He'd gifted her with everything she'd ever wanted: a husband and family, and now his love. There was nothing else she needed or desired.

When she started cramping again, Esther didn't want to draw his attention. But the pain worsened, and she got up to take her medicine in the kitchen before she moved to her favorite chair and ottoman.

"Are you *oll recht*?" Joshua's concerned voice startled her.

She gasped. "*Ja*," she murmured and shut her eyes. "I took something. I'll be fine."

He shifted to face her. "Don't suffer in silence, Esther. Please always tell me when you don't feel well."

Esther could just make out his features in the darkness. "I will. I'm sorry. I didn't want to disrupt your rest."

With her promise from last night echoing in her head, she woke with a startled gasp the next morning. She'd slept too late, and she had sugar doughnuts to make. She heard Joshua moving about in the kitchen. What kind of wife was she that she didn't already have breakfast ready for her husband and children on Christmas morning? Esther hurriedly washed up then dressed in a royal blue tab dress with a white cape and apron. She took great pains to make herself look presentable, with her hair neatly pinned in place under her head covering.

The delicious aroma of coffee was in the air when she entered the kitchen. Her husband was nowhere to be seen. He couldn't have gone far, she reasoned, since he'd made the brew using a French press rather than their metal pot. And he'd added coffee to a thermal pitcher to keep it hot. Much to her surprise, he'd set the table for breakfast.

After tying on a patchwork cooking apron, Esther pulled

out the ingredients to make the donuts. The back door opened with a bang as the wind blew inside.

"*Gut mariga, liebchen,*" Joshua said as he entered with a box in his hand. "No need to cook breakfast this morning. I have powdered-sugar crullers I bought yesterday from Kings."

"You bought doughnuts?" she asked, surprised by his thoughtfulness.

"*Ja,* I told you—you work too hard. Today is for relaxing and enjoying our family." He set the box on the table. "They're a little chilly since I kept them in our buggy."

Esther collected the ingredients she'd taken out and began to put them away. Joshua was quick to help her. "You made special coffee for Christmas."

He nodded. "It wasn't hard. Fannie showed me how to make it and lent me her French press. Would you like a cup?" She nodded and he quickly took out a mug and filled it, leaving enough room for the milk and sugar they both preferred.

"Please sit," he said as he handed her her coffee.

"Joshua—"

"Sit, *frau.* The birthday girl should be able to enjoy her coffee while our children sleep."

"You remembered," she breathed as she obeyed his instructions.

"Of course I remember." He regarded her with warmth. "I have something for you. I don't think our *kinner* will be interested so I can give it to you now, or you may wait until later if you want." He raised his eyebrows.

She grinned. "I like to enjoy coffee with you."

He poured himself a cup and joined her at the table. "Take your time. There is no rush. We have the whole day ahead of us."

They enjoyed their time together while the children were

still asleep in bed. "I'll be right back," he told her a little bit later. Then, bundled against the winter weather, he left the house. She figured he'd gone out to check on their horses. Esther didn't move while he was gone but kept an ear out for sounds from the back rooms.

Joshua was back quickly with a medium-sized, wrapped package.

She studied it. "What is it?"

"Only one way to find out," he said, settling it on her lap.

Esther wrinkled her nose as she tried to guess what was inside the decorated box. "You're not going to give me a hint?"

He laughed. "Not even a small one, *frau*. Now open it before the moment is lost and the girls come running to find us."

She gently pulled off the birthday wrap. The box underneath felt heavy but gave her no clue what was inside. Esther shook it once and then again, but the contents made no sound.

"Esther." He shook his head. "Just open it."

And so she did. Then she gasped at what she found. Inside were two large pieces of dress fabric, one a lively spring green and the other a lovely shade of sky blue. "I love them. So much. *Danki*, Joshua. There looks like enough yardage of each color to make garments for the girls and me."

Esther decided to be brave and kissed him. When she pulled back, she saw he looked pleased that she'd taken the initiative.

"Dat! Esther!" Leah's voice alerted them that the girls were awake.

He grinned. "Made it in the nick of time, *mein* wife."

"Merry Christmas!" Magda entered, holding her baby brothers' hands.

Leah trailed behind her, grinning. "It's Christmas!"

"*Ja,* it is," Joshua said. "We have crullers for breakfast, but maybe you'd like cereal first."

"Do we have to have cereal?" Leah whined.

"It's a special day," he said, "so *nay,* you don't."

Everyone scrambled to sit. While Joshua refilled their coffee mugs, Esther poured each child a glass of milk. Then they all ate long powdered-sugar crullers, humming their enjoyment in between bites.

"Let's go into the living room," Joshua said when they were done.

Esther went to the storage chest to get the gifts she'd made them. She gave their daughters their new black bonnets, and they beamed at her, pleased to have ones like hers. Then she gave the twins their navy blue scarves, wrapping them around their necks, making faces to hear their laughter.

Then she handed Joshua his Christmas gift. He gazed at her warmly as he shook it, causing her to chuckle as he mimicked her actions earlier with her birthday gift box. Then he unwrapped it and saw the scarf she'd made for him. It felt soft yet heavy. "This is perfect," he told her. "Better than my old one. This will keep me warmer." His smile for her made her feel giddy.

Esther brought out another box. "This is for our family," she said.

"Can I open it?" Leah asked.

"*May* I open it," Esther corrected with a gentle smile. "*Ja,* you may."

"What is it?" Magda said when she saw the unwrapped gift.

Joshua smiled at her. "It's a game called Aggravation. We can play it together."

Esther was pleased with everyone's reaction. She had two more small gifts for her husband. "Something you need, and something you'll like." She gave them to him.

"Gloves!" he exclaimed, looking pleased. "And chocolates." He stood and pulled her against his side. "*Danki, liebchen*," he whispered in her ear. His sudden grin took her by surprise. "Now for your Christmas gift." When she opened her mouth to object, he held up his hand to stop her. "That fabric is for your birthday. Wait here a minute." He left the room and returned several minutes later. "Children, it's snowing outside!"

"It is!" Magda exclaimed.

"Can we go sledding, Dat?"

Eyeing them with affection, he nodded. "After we eat. The snow isn't going to melt quickly, and the more we get the better the ride. Grossdaddi Jonas brought over my old toboggan yesterday. We'll have fun with it."

"I can't wait," Leah said with a grin.

"Me either," Magda added.

As she listened to the girls' excitement about taking a toboggan ride later in the day, Esther felt an overwhelming happiness at being here with her family...the husband she loved and who loved her...the children she'd always wanted, who felt like her own. This Christmas Day and birthday promised to be her best yet.

"Esther." Joshua reached for her hand, tugging her from her chair and leading her to the kitchen. "Merry Christmas, *Liebchen*."

She froze when she saw a large, plastic-covered item in the middle of the room. "When did you...how did you get this here?" she asked, her curiosity rising as she approached it. She eyed her gift. "What is it?"

"Something you need," he said. "Just pull off the plastic wrapping."

Esther tugged off the plastic. She gasped. "A sewing machine?"

He nodded. "You needed one of your own so that you don't need to keep borrowing your *mam*'s."

"Joshua." Tears filled her eyes as she met his gaze. "I don't know what to say."

"Do you like it?" He softened his expression as he continued to study her.

"I love it!" she cried. "But not as much as I love you."

"*Gut* answer, *liebchen*." He pulled her into his arms and she sighed, feeling safe and secure with her husband. And at that moment, there was no other place she'd rather be.

Epilogue

"**M**am!"

Esther heard the loud thunder of feet against hardwood floor, indicating the arrival of one or both twins. Jacob skidded to a halt when he saw her on the living room sofa.

"What is it, Jacob?" She examined him thoroughly for any injuries. "Is anything wrong? Are you hurt?"

Jacob shook his head. It was hard for her to believe that the boys were four now. It had been two years since she'd become their mother. She still felt emotional whenever she recalled the first time the twins had called her *Mam*, the title quickly adopted by their daughters on the same day.

"Jacob!" Magda entered the living room, searching for her brother. "I told you not to bother her," she said with a huff when she saw him. "She's resting for two now."

Jacob blinked. "Two?"

Esther's daughter's blue gaze gleamed with amusement. "*Ja*. I told you… Mam is having a baby."

"I'm going to be a big *bruder*," Jacob said, puffing up his chest.

Esther smiled. "*Ja*, you are."

"Jacob." Magda sighed. "*Dat* wants you in his workshop."

"*Okey*." The boy rushed from the room.

It was a warm spring day, and Esther had left the back door open to allow in fresh air. Sounds from outside filtered easily through the screened outer door, allowing her to hear her son as he raced toward the barn. "I'm coming, Dat! I'm coming!" Last summer Joshua had built an addition to their barn, adding a room where he enjoyed working on woodcrafts and furniture. He was currently finishing up a cradle for their baby, who was due in three weeks.

Esther's oldest remained at her side. Magda was eight now, and a big help to her in the kitchen. "Vadder wants to know if you are feeling *oll recht*."

"Tell him I'm fine." Esther rubbed her extended belly, enjoying her baby bump.

She'd never thought she'd be here, anticipating the birth of her child. Until her visit to the doctor during their first January together had changed everything. The female physician had explained that endometriosis couldn't be diagnosed by a simple exam. Esther's last doctor should have performed laparoscopic surgery if the presence of endometrial lesions was suspected. It was the only way to get a good look inside her abdomen.

Esther was glad she'd consented to see Dr. Brown, an experienced gynecologist, who had moved to New Berne two years prior. The woman had immediately ordered an ultrasound and a CT scan for her. When they'd returned for the results, she and Joshua had received news they'd never expected. Her last doctor had been wrong. She had fibroids, not endometriosis.

She and Joshua had asked numerous questions, and Dr. Brown had answered each one patiently, which made it easier for her and Joshua to decide the best course for her health.

Three weeks later Esther had undergone a myomectomy

in which the fibroids were removed. The procedure went well for her. During her six-week recovery time, their parents stepped in to help with the children. Now it was two years later, and they were having a baby, a blessing that would be a new sister for their daughters and sons. Everything good that had happened in her life was *Gott*'s will.

And she'd never been happier.

Joshua entered the room minutes after Magda had left. "Are you sure you're *oll recht*?"

Esther extended her hand to the man she loved. Her husband clasped her fingers gently, keeping hold as he sat down on the sofa beside her. "I have never felt better, Joshua," she said softly. "Please don't worry. Everything will go smoothly. I have complete faith that the Lord wants us to have this child."

He managed a smile. "You will call me if you need me?"

She picked up the cell phone lying on the cushion beside her. "And you have yours, I have no doubt."

He nodded. "Have I told you lately how happy I am that you're my wife?"

"Not in the last two hours." She smirked. "But I never get tired of hearing it." Esther reached up to tug playfully on Joshua's beard, then laughed when he arched an eyebrow as he cradled her fingers against his chin.

His brown eyes went soft. "I love you, *liebchen*. I'm happy I married you."

"I love you, Joshua." She ran her fingers from his cheek to his forehead.

"Mam! Dat!" Leah yelled from inside the house after the screened door slammed. "The twins are ruining everything!"

With a sigh, Joshua stood. "I'd better see what her problem is."

"It's probably nothing." Esther grinned. "You know how dramatic Leah can get when it comes to her *bruders*."

He bent down for a kiss and to trail the knuckles of one hand across her cheek. "I'll be back soon."

She held his fingers against her skin briefly. "I'm counting on it, husband." Her baby kicked in her belly, a feeling she loved sharing with Joshua whenever it happened when they were together. She smiled and caressed her big belly. Her unborn daughter was active today.

Thank you, Lord, for your gifts. I shall forever be grateful for the family You have given and the new life I've been allowed to carry. Please continue to guide and bless us. In this Your name. Amen.

Two weeks later, baby Sarah Anna Miller was born. Astonished at first, Joshua looked at Esther with pure joy after she suggested Anna as a middle name for their baby daughter. Anna, the name of her husband's late wife.

Esther lovingly studied the child in her arms, deciding that Sarah and the baby's father shared the same facial features. When she looked up, her husband's eyes were filled with love for her and for the life they had created together. Their brood was now five instead of four. And she and Joshua couldn't be happier.

* * * * *

*If you enjoyed this story,
be sure to check out
Rebecca Kertz's previous book*
His Forgotten Amish Love
now available from Love Inspired!

Discover more at LoveInspired.com.

Dear Reader,

Welcome to New Berne, the home of the Miller, Troyer and Fisher families! Joshua Miller returns to his childhood Amish village to be closer to his family. His wife was killed in a car accident, which left him an injured widower with four children. With his father's help, he settles into his new home, grateful that his family is there for him. But then his father urges him to find a wife who will be a mother for Joshua's young children. Joshua will do anything for his little ones, but he struggles with the idea of doing his duty of acquiring a new wife. His father suggests a matchmaker, but Joshua tells him that he will find his bride once he's ready. He is still grieving for the woman he loved and lost. Eventually, however, he realizes he can stay faithful to his late wife's memory as long as the woman he weds will agree to accept that theirs will be a marriage of convenience only.

Esther King has been cleaning house for Joshua Miller since he moved into his new home. One day, out of the blue, the man asks her to marry him and explains the conditions of his offer. Esther accepts his proposal for secret reasons of her own. She's always wanted a husband and children but never expected the reality of having a family.

Would she regret wedding a man who can't get over his grief? Will the secret she is carrying eventually destroy their new relationship?

New Berne in Lancaster County, Pennsylvania, is a great place to visit. If you haven't stopped by previously, you can still meet other residents there in my other novels—*Lov-*

ing Her Amish Neighbor, *The Widow's Secret Past* and *His Forgotten Amish Love*.

I wish you good health, much love and true happiness.

Blessings and light,
Rebecca Kertz